PENGUIN BOOKS

A CHANGE FOR THE BETTER

Susan Hill was born in Scarborough, Yorkshire, in 1942. She was educated at grammar schools there and in Coventry, and studied at King's College, London. Her works include *Gentleman and Ladies*, *I'm the King of the Castle* (Somerset Maugham Prize), *The Albatross and Other Stories* (John Llewelyn Rhys Memorial Prize), *Strange Meeting*, *The Bird of Night* (Whitbread Award), *A Bit of Singing and Dancing*, *In the Springtime of the Year*, *The Woman in Black* and *Lanterns Across the Snow*, as well as the illustrated *Shakespeare Country*, *The Spirit of the Cotswolds*, *Through the Garden Gate* and *Through the Kitchen Window*. She has also written books for children, *One Night at a Time*, *Mother's Magic* and *Can It Be True?* (Smarties Prize), and two autobiographical books, *The Magic Apple Tree* and *Family*. In addition she has edited Thomas Hardy's *The Distracted Preacher and Other Tales* for the Penguin Classics and is a regular broadcaster and book reviewer.

Susan Hill is married to the Shakespeare scholar Stanley Wells. They have two daughters and live in the Oxfordshire countryside.

Susan Hill

A Change for the Better

Penguin Books

For David

PENGUIN BOOKS

Published by the Penguin Group
Penguin Books Ltd, 27 Wrights Lane, London W8 5TZ, England
Penguin Books USA Inc., 375 Hudson Street, New York, New York 10014, USA
Penguin Books Australia Ltd, Ringwood, Victoria, Australia
Penguin Books Canada Ltd, 10 Alcorn Avenue, Toronto, Ontario, Canada M4V 3B2
Penguin Books (NZ) Ltd, 182–190 Wairau Road, Auckland 10, New Zealand

Penguin Books Ltd, Registered Offices: Harmondsworth, Middlesex, England

First published by Hamish Hamilton Ltd 1969
Published in Penguin Books 1980
10 9 8 7

Printed in England by Clays Ltd, St Ives plc
Set in Linotype Pilgrim

Chapter One

'WHY, today is the twenty-second of November,' said Mrs Deirdre Fount to her mother, Mrs Winifred Oddicott, as they passed by the Prince of Wales Hotel. 'Now you surely cannot have forgotten what happens today!'

Mrs Winifred Oddicott lowered her head against the east wind, but said nothing.

'Today the Carpenters return home. How exciting, and what a lot they will have to tell us all! I am sure I can scarcely wait.'

'Are we expecting to see them, then? Has something been planned?'

'Oh, we are sure to *see* them, mother. They will come into the shop, or we shall meet somewhere, or perhaps I might . . .'

'Yes?'

'Oh, well . . . But anyway, she is sure to come into the shop, as I have said. Yes, it is all very exciting.'

Mrs Oddicott looked sideways at her only daughter, a sharp curious look.

'Clearly you have been thinking a good deal about the Carpenters,' she said, 'when I had, I must confess, quite forgotten about them. They do not interest me at all, they can scarcely be called *friends* of ours. But I see that, for you, their doings hold a great fascination.'

'No, no. But it is something to think of, something new, an event. We need an event, every now and again.'

'Do we?'

Deirdre Fount was unable to reply.

'James must wear his mackintosh to go to his lesson this afternoon,' said Mrs Oddicott.

'Yes. I daresay he will remember,' said Mrs Fount, the mother of James. 'I have left him a note.'

A gust of wind rippled the hems of their coats and seemed to steer them like boats, gently towards the corner, where they would turn away from the Esplanade and into Norfolk Terrace.

They walked in precisely the same way, mother and daughter, with a pinched, corseted movement of the hips. In the past, Deirdre Fount had tried to eradicate the likeness, to move differently. It was enough to look into the mirror and see her own face settling more and more into the likeness of her mother's. But now, she had resigned herself to the walk, as to many other things. And today it did not matter, for today she could think about the homecoming of Major and Mrs Bertram Carpenter.

'We are late,' said Mrs Winifred Oddicott. Her daughter began to walk a little more quickly.

From her balcony flat and her wheelchair, the rich Miss Prug watched them go, down the Esplanade and around the corner.

'They are late,' she said, 'Mrs Fount and Mrs Oddicott. It is a quarter to nine already.'

'Already!' said Mrs Christie, her companion, entering with the breakfast trolley and the pekinese dog.

From St Thomas's church tower, the clock began to chime.

'And how like her mother that girl is growing! They could be taken for sisters. Ah, I see that I have a letter from the nuns!'

'She is only thirty-nine.'

'Deirdre Fount?'

'Thirty-nine years old, yes.'

'It is hard to believe and sad to see.'

'Well, she has the young boy.'

Miss Prug raised her eyebrows, buttered a triangle of toast. 'No,' she said, 'you are quite wrong. *She* does not have the boy.'

'Then she has only herself to blame. There was a choice to be made and she made it, this is the life she has preferred. She is a fully-grown and responsible woman.'

'I think,' said Miss Violet Prug, slitting open her letter, 'I think that there is more to it than that.'

The idea came into her mind quite suddenly. They were stocktaking, and she was checking on the number of cards of press-studs (assorted) in the third drawer from the top, on the left. It dropped into her empty mind like a coin in a slot, and at once she was excited. And ashamed of the idea. And dismissed it as ridiculous. But was surprised that it had not come to her before.

The idea was: The Carpenters may invite me to their table for dinner one evening.

The Carpenters summoned people to dine at their table in the Prince of Wales Hotel where they were resident, rather as the Captain of a ship summons his passengers. It was a great honour, most selectively bestowed, and much coveted. Mrs Deirdre Fount had not been asked so far, but now, the idea came to her that because the Carpenters were back and would be asking a number of people to their table over the next few weeks, she, Deirdre Fount, would be chosen.

She did not tell her mother about the idea, but only said aloud, 'There are plenty left. We need not re-order for some while.'

But her idea had altered the complexion of the day, given her new hope and some cheerfulness.

'Yes,' her mother said. Mrs Oddicott knelt at one of the lower drawers and counted interlock vests. Among such things they passed their lives from nine each morning until five-thirty each night. Cami-knickers, dress-shields, safety-pins (small, gilt), safety-pins (large, silver), tape measures, bodkins, zip fasteners, french chalk, replacement suspenders in white, flesh-pink and, until recently, also in black.

'*Black?*' Mrs Winifred Oddicott had said, when Deirdre Fount had mentioned it. 'Black? Oh, surely not!'

'Now, mother, you must put away these ideas about black corsets and black underwear. It is very fashionable now, it . . .'

'It may well be *fashionable*!'

'And respectable, too. Quite. It is accepted. We are here, I think, to provide a complete service and so we must extend our range and stock black replacement suspenders.'

'I wonder, dear. I do not like to seem old-fashioned, and I do not try to argue with you for argument's sake. I only wonder, whether the ladies of Westbourne . . . Well, I should not wear black.'

'New people come into the town and in the summer we have visitors, fashions change.'

'We are a traditional drapery shop, Deirdre, we have always prided ourselves upon that fact. Customers like ours do not want novelty and change.'

'But if they want black replacement suspenders, well, that is what we should be able to provide. There is such a thing . . .' and Deirdre Fount had begun to flush a little, conscious of her own stubbornness '. . . as a happy medium. Let us be practical and let us not convey a *dowdy* image of ourselves, mother.'

Afterwards, she had been proud of the way she had stood up for what she thought right. It proves, she thought, that when I need to, I can be firm. Though she knew that it was only over such trivialities as the stocking of black replacement suspenders. On major issues she had never been firm, never stood her ground or won the day. Over the suspenders, however, she had won. Only to be proved quite wrong, for they had not sold, they had lingered on in a bottom drawer, while flesh-pink and white were continually re-ordered. Mrs Winifred Oddicott had said nothing more upon the subject, only opened the drawer from time to time and turned the bundles over pointedly.

'We are not a *modern* shop,' she would say, 'there will be no revolving displays of button-cards here, no knocking out of windows and streamlining of the shop front. This is our image, we provide a service in the setting our customers have always preferred.'

Though their customers were never consulted. But that was Mrs Winifred Oddicott's creed, which she repeated and repeated. In her heart, Deirdre Fount despised it, and knew it to be true. And this Monday morning, she counted the needles and the pins and the reels of black button thread and made up the order list for the embroidery silks traveller and at times, glancing out of the shop window into Pavilion Street, thought, dear God, I am thirty-nine years old already and that is almost forty. I am nine years divorced, albeit most decently, and I have an eleven-year-old son. I count the packets of pins. I am my mother's daughter. Is this to be all?

Mrs Winifred Oddicott shut the last drawer firmly and rose to her feet.

'After what you said this morning,' she told her daughter loudly, 'I am afraid that you are cherishing *hopes* . . .'

'Hopes? What are you thinking of, mother? Oh, now we are quite out of olive green bias binding!'

'Hopes that the Carpenters will invite you to one of their evenings, will have you to dinner at the Prince of Wales Hotel.'

She is a witch, thought Deirdre Fount. I have said nothing, I have longed and hoped and all in secret, for I would never let my mother know my thoughts. She is a witch, and now it is all ruined.

Aloud, she said, 'Why what perfect nonsense!'

'Oh yes, quite. That is exactly what it is. You will never be in favour with the Carpenters, dear, however much you may have visited her during her illness this last summer.'

'I went to see if I could be of use, that was all. I have no wish to insinuate myself anywhere.'

'I am very glad to hear it. I would not have you disappointed, Deirdre. Now – is there much call for olive green bias binding?'

Deirdre Fount, growing more, not less vulnerable with the onset of middle age, trembled with frustration and the need to cry.

In the cold classrooms of Westbourne Priors School, the lights went on before two o'clock, because of the overcast November sky, and in Form 11A, the voice of Robin Broom stumbled on.

'Having crossed the river – no, the water . . . *sea* . . .'

'River, Broom, as you were. River.'

'Yes, sir. Having crossed the river, the army of Caesar made for . . .'

'The *what?*'

'No, I mean Caesar's army made for the open country.'

James Fount stared down at the book and thought that it would most probably rain and he would have to wear his mackintosh and boots to walk up to Cliff House for his lesson. Next, he thought about his father, which was difficult, because there could be no substance to his thoughts, they did not centre upon the definite recollection of a face and a body. He had never seen his father – not, at least, since the age of two months, nor was that father ever spoken of. Once a year, perhaps, until recently, James Fount had wondered about him, in a detached and largely uninterested way. Now, he was eleven years old and the thoughts came often. He tried to picture the man, to give him a place in some scale of standards, but he did not have any idea of how his father would think, in what way his mind would be likely to work. He knew *why* he now had no father, firm and final reasons had been supplied by his grandmother, Mrs Winifred Oddicott.

Only now, secretly during a Latin lesson, or when walking home past the tall, white houses of the Esplanade, or pinning dead butterflies on to a card, he thought of his father, wondered about him and tried to imagine what they might say to one another if they met.

'In time to come, they would establish winter quarters and . . .'

'Oh, sit down, Broom, for heaven's sake! Fount?'

'Yes, sir. The time came when they had to establish winter quarters and . . .'

'At least you know what you're about. Go on, boy.'

James Fount went on and thought no more about his father that day.

'How nice that it is all the same, dear, just the same,' said Mrs Flora Carpenter, and looked out of the wide windows that afforded them their coveted and costly view of Westbourne Bay.

Her husband struggled with the tying of his shoelaces and she dared not ask him if he required help.

'Well of course it is all just the same, I cannot see the point of that remark at all. Did you expect it to be different?'

'Oh, no. No, I did not.'

'We have been travelling about, seeing this and that, the world has been passing before our eyes and so you have become disorientated and expect everything to be different. But these rooms have remained in our absence, the life of the hotel goes on and only the cleaners have been in here.'

'Yes, dear. Of course.'

'Or I hope only the cleaners! Now *there* is a thought, Flora. The management may slyly let this suite in our absence, and in spite of the uninterrupted payments I make, and the fact that some of this furniture is our own. That would not surprise me, now I come to think, they will go to any lengths, you know, to see extra money coming in, all is grist to their mill.'

Mrs Flora Carpenter wondered if he was always like this, so suspicious and irritable, if he had been like this as a young man of twenty-two when she had married him. She could not remember. Perhaps old age had brought out his true character, or formed a new one. But it was her task to soothe and reassure him, to help him accept.

So she said now, 'I am sure that Mr Plumb would never tolerate such a thing.'

'It is not Plumb, it has nothing whatsoever to do with Plumb, did you not know that?'

'He is the Hotel Manager, dear.'

'Yes, and that is all. He does not own the place, he is only an employee of as much standing in the eyes of the Company as the bell boy. If it is their policy to . . .'

'Oh, but I do not think it can be.'

Major Bertram Carpenter rattled the pages of the *Daily Telegraph*, irritably, unable to hold up his arms for very long, and creasing the paper awkwardly, so that it was quite spoiled and, before she could read it, she would have to spend ten minutes refolding and assembling it in order. Once, she had said, let us order two papers and then we may enjoy them simultaneously and undisturbed. But he had raved about the waste of money and been hurt that she did not feel herself able to enjoy a newspaper after he had read it. It had taken some days for her to calm him once more.

The backs of his hands were knotted with upstanding veins and the skin was transparent under the West Indies tan. He was seventy-three years old, of excellent health and evil temper.

'The place is not what it was,' he said to her confidently, 'it is no longer a family concern.'

'I know, dear.'

'It is owned by a large public company, they have a chain of hotels and word never reaches the ears of the man at the top, he sits all day behind a closed door.'

Mrs Flora Carpenter had a vision of discreet corridors in some important building, with blue carpet and rosewood panelling and small notices of white on black, PRIVATE, and CHAIRMAN.

'Well, I shall soon find out and have something to say.'

'Now, Bertram, there is no evidence of any kind, there is nothing at all to lead you to believe that other people have been staying in our rooms.'

'Ha!'

'None at all. Everything is quite in order, quite as it should be. You have no reason to complain.'

'Three months, that is a long time to be away, you know.'

'Yes, dear.'

'A lot can happen in three months, when one's back is turned.'

She was all but losing her patience with him and would have left the room to prevent herself answering sharply to his foolishness, when he said, 'I have not forgotten that tomorrow is November the twenty-third. November the twenty-third is the anniversary of our engagement. You need not think that I have forgotten.'

And so she did not leave, she smiled across at him and leaned to pick up her glasses and embroidery frame, and let herself remember that he had been a good husband, a strong and thoughtful man, many were worse, and so the morning wore on until coffee time. Mrs Carpenter thought of the gentle rhythm of the ship, to which she had grown so accustomed, and the gaiety of the West Indies. Her own skin was a rich brown, for she had spent much of every day on the First Class deck, and read many books, made many friends. She thought, I shall never go there again, never again experience such sunshine to soothe my old bones.

'Oh, but it is nice to be home and settled,' she said to the girl who brought up the coffee tray, for she did not ever wish to think dissatisfied thoughts. 'It is nice to be quiet and stay for some time in one place. We shall have nothing to disturb us now, until Christmas.'

'I'd never have come back,' said the waitress, clearing books to make room for the tray, 'I can't understand you, not in this weather as well.'

'Oh, but there is much to be said for it, you know. It is so soft and subtle, and the sunshine can be very monotonous, very harsh. One grows tired of it, day after day.'

'Catch me!'

'Well, you are young. I will settle for my life here, now, everything nice and quiet.'

'Yes, when the conference is over you will.'

'Oh!' said Mrs Flora Carpenter, much dismayed, 'is there to be another conference? We thought we had so nicely avoided them all and my husband does hate it so, it makes him unsettled. They are even worse for him than the summer visitors. Is it . . .' she paused and lowered her voice a fraction, 'is it *political?*'

'No, trade, I think, but I'm not sure what. Will that be all, Madam?'

'Thank you,' said Mrs Carpenter, taking out a handkerchief to cope with the hot handles.

'Bertram, there is to be a conference, dear. Did you hear that? Now I hope you will not make too much of a fuss.'

In the chair opposite, her husband was asleep, his mouth open to show an even line of false teeth.

Then I will not tell him, decided Mrs Carpenter, I will keep the peace for a while longer, and let him find out as he may. For her own part and quite in secret, she found the winter conferences rather exciting. So many people came, one simply never *knew* . . .

Major Bertram Carpenter awoke with a start and the *Daily Telegraph* slid to the floor.

'Now I shall tell you what is to be done,' he said, 'I shall tell you what I have decided.' He took his cup of coffee from her and set it down perilously upon the arm of the chair.

'Yes, dear? What is that?'

'We shall invite that young woman, that Mrs Fount. We shall have *her* to our next dinner party.'

Mrs Flora Carpenter, who was considerably surprised but not at all displeased, said nothing.

'I shall talk to her about the trip, describe foreign countries and customs, for she has been nowhere, seen nothing, it will interest her.'

'Do you think so, Bertram?'

'Certainly. She will appreciate it all.'

'Perhaps, yes . . .'

'Well, where is your pencil, where is your diary? Come along, Flora, let us have a list made.'

Mrs Flora Carpenter reached for her crocodile handbag. One afternoon on the ship, cruising towards the Bahamas, he had woken up and said, 'I have made up my mind, there are to be no more dinner parties. People have started to take us for granted, it must come to an end. We shall go into retirement and dine alone.'

And she had not contradicted him, only been saddened and hoped very much that he would change his mind. And now, here was a delight, he must have known of her disappointment and planned to make it up to her. Happily, she opened her diary and headed the new list for a dinner party with the name Mrs Deirdre Fount.

'Surely that is not *another* slice of bread you are cutting for yourself?' asked Mrs Winifred Oddicott of her daughter. They lunched in the little dark sitting room at the back of the shop, on boiled or scrambled eggs, slices of cold ham and tomatoes, bought pies or, as today, soup, bread and cheese. Deirdre Fount would have preferred to eat the five and sixpenny, three-course lunch with coffee ninepence extra, at the Laurel Leaf Café immediately opposite. It was clean and she liked the atmosphere of cafés, they filled her with the hope of unexpected meetings, unfamiliar worlds. A change of surroundings, company and conversation and to be served rather than to serve, all these she would have enjoyed. But her mother did not like cafés, they charged exorbitant prices for small portions, she said, you did not know what went on out of sight in their kitchens, the vegetables were always overcooked and the puddings lumpy. Besides, whoever needed *two* full, cooked meals a day?

But of course, she also said, if that is what you want then go by all means, go. Deirdre Fount did not go but consoled herself with extra slices of bread in the back sitting room.

'You will run to fat, Deirdre, you must be very careful. Our family has a tendency to fatness in later life.'

'There is plenty of time for me to worry about that, I am young and active and really rather thin.'

'You are almost middle-aged, almost forty, now let us be

honest, dear. It is in middle age that the waistline starts to thicken and the muscles to grow slack. That is also when women start to indulge themselves by way of compensation.'

'Compensation for what?'

Mrs Winifred Oddicott turned her eyes away abruptly and ate from the bowl of soup.

'There are,' she said, after a pause, 'various psychological disturbances – you will discover. Though that is not to say that one should give in, they are to be expected and accepted, *my* mother always said.'

'Oh, good gracious, I am not ready for the menopause yet!'

Mrs Oddicott set her jaw in a tight line. Well, she thought, I will say nothing, I will try and understand. For occasionally, Deirdre Fount would throw in her lot with the young and outspoken, would try to put on a bold, careless front. Perhaps it had to do with the remaining shock of the divorce, or perhaps, after all, it was a trait buried in her character. Mrs Oddicott knew her side of the family to be blameless in that respect, but thought darkly of Gerald, her late husband. The influence of Aubrey Fount, too, should not be forgotten or lightly dismissed. In their three years of marriage, much harm had clearly been done.

So she would ignore these little outbursts of vulgarity, the public use of words like menopause, just as one ignored the swear words of a small child. Both were symptoms of some desire for prominence, the need to be thought shocking, but she, Deirdre's mother, would not be shocked, she would *understand* and be tolerant.

'Well, I suppose, dear,' she said now, brightly, 'that you might always try those little sandwich biscuits in place of lunch. If you did become aware of the extra inches creeping up on you. I have heard they are quite nutritious and very pleasant to eat, in various sweet or savoury flavours . . .'

Deirdre Fount got to her feet so suddenly that she knocked over the chair behind her. I cannot bear it, she thought, I shall go out of my mind.

'I am going to walk down to Hoskins. I have one or two things to buy.' And she escaped into the street before her mother could ask her what the things were or decide to accompany her.

Once there, she turned towards the Esplanade and the sea, away from Hoskins Department Store. If she had not left she thought that she would have shouted and there would have been one of their quarrels, the whole awful pattern would have to be repeated – the bitter recriminations, the attempts at calm, the taunts and even tears, the afternoon of silence and then, inevitably, Deirdre's apology and her mother's generous forgiveness.

She walked very quickly, having only thirty-five minutes to spare, so that she was out of breath when she reached the steps and path down to the Scented Gardens. She saw no one, all the wheelchairs were indoors and even the hardiest of the people from the blind home were within, for the time being, eating lunch and dozing in warm lounges.

The gardens were flowerless except that here and there hung a last, beige rose. Mrs Deirdre Fount sat in one of the shelters, on a wooden bench, and looked down upon flat water lilies in flat ponds.

She would have liked to smoke a cigarette but had brought none. Not that at home they were forbidden, certainly not, for her mother smoked five tipped Kensitas every day of her life. But she passed severe judgement upon women who smoked out of doors or in public places and so, her daughter would have liked to do it now. To join, in the eyes of her mother, those vulgar, common people who were also the women who bought fish and chips and ate them outside, would have been a temporary and illicit delight. That was all, for in truth Deirdre Fount did not much care for the taste of tobacco.

So she was forced to sit, hands folded in her lap, in the bleak gardens, and feel foolish. I should not quarrel, she told herself, I should not behave so childishly, for it is all grist to my mother's mill.

I am glad that I had a son, she thought next (and not for the first time), rather than a daughter. For James will not be in any danger, he will break the chains and get away, establish himself, stand on his own two feet. Not yet, but in ten years or so. James, by the very nature of things, would be saved from his mother. If she had had a daughter, Deirdre Fount knew that she would have been tempted to get her own back, to let the sins be visited, as they had been visited upon her.

They had always been a family of women who knew nothing of and despised men, wanting no part of them, failing with them in all respects.

Mrs Winifred Oddicott had been the youngest child of older parents. At the age of nineteen her mother had told her that all spinsters lived at a disadvantage and indeed, were a shame to their parents, as though they had some flaw as a result of which no man cared to marry them.

'You will do best to marry,' she had said and thereupon had produced the young man she considered suitable. Gerald Oddicott had been impressed by the concerted effort of so many people – for the whole of Winifred's family had been behind the business – to make him one of their number. They like me, he had thought, with some pride, they think I am worth having.

Winifred herself had been uncertain, not only about him but about the idea of marriage. She wanted to go her own way, she said, to prove herself, to be an independent, modern woman. Both ideas were quickly held up to ridicule and then quashed. But she found Gerald Oddicott weak and whey-faced, his jokes irritated her, although his pliable good nature was convenient, for he longed to give her her own way.

Then, after two months of vacillation, she discovered that he had been offered a post in the Indian Civil Service, and at once she saw him in an entirely different light, as one who might, were she not careful, slip through her fingers. He took on all the glamour of a prospective traveller to exotic foreign lands. Winifred Oddicott had panicked, realizing suddenly that she was not a pretty or a clever girl. So she had married him in the end, with something like relief, without love but with a certain youthful willingness to be charmed by the romance of India and by a new and attentive husband.

She had been utterly disappointed. India was hot and enervating and strange, she was afraid of the Indians and intimidated by the whites. Her experiences of sex quickly taught her to despise her husband – and indeed, she supposed, all men – who could be so easily enslaved by such an indignity. For eighteen months she had despised and been bored by him – towards the end of which time she had conceived Deirdre. Two months later, Gerald Oddicott died of typhoid fever. His widow returned to England to give birth and thereafter to nurse a demanding mother through a slow and painful death. She had thankfully relinquished all further contact with the world of men. Had she been able she would, like some god-parents relinquishing the devil and all his works, have done the same on behalf of her daughter. Certainly she tried her best, and lived with her mother and Deirdre and then with Deirdre alone, in a tight, close, female world. Deirdre had, for the most part, succumbed and inclined towards books and music and needlework, brought home no boy-friends or unsuitable magazines, showed no curiosity, beyond what was inevitable, about the world of men.

Then, at the age of twenty-five, she had met Aubrey Fount, and, in one of her bouts of rebellion and inquisitiveness, married him seven weeks later. Disillusionment, separation and the return home to Mrs Oddicott had followed swiftly, together with the birth of James.

Aubrey Fount was a car salesman who wore pin-striped suits and a ginger moustache and he had not, from the beginning, stood a chance. He had married not merely a diffident wife but her mother and a whole tradition of female self-sufficiency. He had panicked, after the excitement of marrying an extremely naïve girl had died down, and looked about for consolation. It was a relief to Mrs Winifred Oddicott, when the divorce proceedings began. Indeed, she had insisted upon them, for she cared very much about the public appearance of things.

Deirdre Fount had never questioned her mother's view of the whole affair, had been entirely influenced in her behaviour and beliefs by Mrs Oddicott. She found it hard now to separate what actually had happened from what her mother had always predicted would happen, and she could remember no conversations with Aubrey, no relationship, no intimacy, that was not intruded upon by her mother. It was as though, having used men to provide them with a status and offspring, to ward off the shames of spinsterhood, they were ready to discard them and sink back into their closed, female society.

Deirdre Fount, conditioned to fear and misunderstand and despise men, had been relieved when the business of the marriage and divorce was over. Her mother helped her to look after the boy James, they moved to Westbourne and bought the shop and the pattern of their daily lives had been formed.

And now, she thought, and now? For she recognized the dissatisfaction and unfulfilled curiosity and doubts within herself, and knew that the next two years would provide her with a last chance. Though a chance of what she could not say. Only after this, after the age of forty, it would surely be too late, James would go away and make his own adult life, her mother would become gradually more and more dependent and set in her ways, and she herself would lose the last optimism of youth and give in to a predictable middle age. Thereafter, the years stretched ahead to the grave and they would be entirely without surprise. She was overcome with the terror of it and got up suddenly from the hard bench, in her anxiety to be free, to have some mystery left. She would not, she could not . . .

To her own alarm, she found herself thinking about Aubrey Fount, and trying to fit together the look of his face in her mind. It was difficult and she felt guilty. One night, she had taken a tiny passport photograph of him, secretly kept, out of a locked drawer and stared at it in her bedroom. She felt nothing at all, there was no life there, but then she remembered having read in some story that the way to bring a photograph to life was to hold it up to a mirror. Somehow, the change of angle made the face appear suddenly and unexpectedly real, as though seen for the first time. She had done this and frightened herself, for it was true, it happened, and she looked into the living face of the man to whom she had been married. At once, she had burned the tiny square of card in the heart of the garden bonfire.

Now all that is past, she told herself, past and dead and it has nothing to do with you, do not make the silly mistake of thinking that your life might have been different, that things were not for the best. If he returned you would not want him, it was all a mistake and it is now forgotten. She began to walk slowly back up the winding cliff path. What would my life have been, she wondered, if my mother had died when I was a girl? How would I then have developed? But she knew that it was not of her own mother that she was most afraid, it was of the world and how it judged her. What do people say of me, she thought, how am I regarded? What bitter or pitying or puzzled remarks do they all make? 'There goes Deirdre Fount with her mother. How long her skirts are, how dowdy her suits, how flat her chest, how unfashionable her hair!' That was what she most feared, the old women watching from balconies and hotel terraces, coming into the shop to buy needles and observing her from the other side of the counter. There were the smart parents, too, of James's friends at Westbourne Priors School.

But what was there to do, how could anything be changed? She had reached the end of the Esplanade, where the north-east wind cut across her face and the war memorial clock showed ten minutes past two. Now, I am late and what is more, I have no parcels in my hands, it is clear that I have not been to Hoskins store at all. Oh, the questions I shall have to endure! She walked swiftly and she wanted to cry out, to push back the tide of her own dissatisfied thoughts, to be docile and happy and settled in her knowledge of the future.

James Fount opened the front door with his own key and put the key back carefully into the brown leather purse, before walking into the silent house.

On the round table in the dining-room was a place mat with a maroon border and a laminated, heat-proof centre picturing a Redouté rose. On the mat, a pink plate, with two cheese sandwiches, a chocolate biscuit, an apple. Beside the mat, a glass of milk. On the armchair nearest the door lay his music case and his flute. And a note.

DO NOT FORGET MACKINTOSH AND BOOTS IN CASE OF RAIN.

His mother's writing. There was often a note and the wording was predictable. James Fount sat down to eat his tea. I do not like the habit of eating in the kitchen, Mrs Winifred Oddicott always said. I make an exception of weekday breakfast, for then, time is to be saved. But James should be brought up in a civilized manner and eat his tea properly in the dining room, whether he is alone or not.

Once, James Fount had been to Morrison's house and the Morrisons ate every meal in the kitchen because of there being so many of them and having irregular hours and a baby who threw food about. He had liked it and been unsettled by it, too. He had never mentioned the experience at home.

He enjoyed returning home to the house empty of his mother and grandmother, and having to eat his tea in the dining room could not spoil it. Today, because of his flute lesson, his time alone was shorter and had to be carefully savoured. Though the lesson, for different reasons, was to be savoured too.

James Fount began to eat his way through the chocolate biscuit.

Chapter Two

Mr Plumb walked down the long empty corridors of the Prince of Wales Hotel, past the tall mirrors that returned him a satisfying image of himself: a stout man, hair receding, only forty-six years of age and conscious of his responsibilities. He walked past the double doors of the Blue Ballroom and the burgundy-coloured Axminster carpet stretched before him, yard after yard.

'In the Grand Tradition,' the guide-book had it, 'the Prince of Wales at Westbourne is one of the finest hotels in England.'

Past the conference room and the first-floor Sun Lounge and on, towards the great, curving staircase, walked Mr Plumb, master of his estate.

At the head of the staircase, he came face to face with Major Bertram Carpenter, out of breath.

'Ah, there you are, sir, there you are! They told me I would find you in your office and you were *not* in your office. I have been all about the hotel.'

'I am sorry, Major. If you had only waited, they would have rung round for me, they . . .'

'There was no one to ring round, all were busily engaged elsewhere, or off duty or eating lunch.'

A change of course being the only line of defence, Mr Plumb said, 'And how may I help you, Major? Is something wrong? What do you require?'

'A straight answer to a straight question, thank you. We pay our way here, I think, meet all our bills promptly, give no trouble.'

'Why of course, there is surely no question of . . .'

'No, there is not and so there can be no possible excuse, can there?'

'For?'

'What I want to know is, who uses our private suite when we are away? What visitors do you import, on the side, Mr Plumb? In fact ...' and struck by the joke he was just to make, Major Carpenter began to lift himself up and down gently, on the balls of his feet, consumed with mirth '... in fact, it is a case of "who's been sitting in *my* chair?"' Major Carpenter was not accustomed to making jokes. His face cracked and creased, he wheezed with elderly laughter. Mr Plumb smiled frigidly, as was his duty.

'There is absolutely no question of it, Major, nobody occupies your private suite, nobody sits in your chair, as you put it. I cannot think how you have come to suspect ...'

'Just a thought, just an idea. I know you hotel people, always anxious to make a swift penny. It is not as though we pay a lower rate when absent, the charges remain the same. Exorbitant.'

'Is there something missing from your rooms, Major Carpenter, something damaged or disarranged? I will speak to the cleaners at once.'

'No need to pass the buck to the cleaners, nothing wrong with the cleaners, perfectly satisfactory. *You* are the manager, it is your responsibility.'

'Major Carpenter, I do not care for your tone of voice, for the way you throw doubt upon my capabilities. If you have ...'

'There is no need to take that attitude, no need at all. Matters have to be broached, I always speak plainly. Well, never mind, never mind, I suppose in these days it is all one can expect from a hotel managed by a public company and so is merely one of a chain.'

Major Carpenter strode off down the burgundy corridor, batting the *Daily Telegraph* impatiently against his trouser leg, stooping forward. It is all part of my day's work, thought Mr Plumb the manager, watching him go. People are difficult, appreciation does not come as a matter of course. He began to descend the wide staircase. But I am conscientious, my conduct is beyond reproach. It is something if I am accused lightly by such a man as Major Carpenter. I am in a position of great responsibility and sorely tried.

Out of irritation and anxious to restore public faith in his position, he spoke most sharply to one of the girls from the kitchen, as he passed by the doors. Behind his back, the girl stuck out her tongue.

Major Bertram Carpenter took the lift to his suite on the fourth floor and found his wife sitting quietly with her embroidery and the radio's Morning Story. 'Well, I have settled matters,' he said, 'I have told the man what is what, it won't happen again.'

'I do not think, dear, that it really happened this time.'

'Of course it did not! But you cannot be too careful, we do not want to become the sort of people who lock the stable door after the horse has bolted.'

Mr Ralph Porlock drank his beer. They did not as a rule exchange a great deal of conversation. James Fount knew very little about his teacher and did not altogether understand him. But he liked it here, liked the freedom and strangeness of it and the way in which he was treated. There were no curtains in the gallery, only wide windows and below, in the darkness, the sound of the sea.

'I cannot imagine what you do up there, or what he can have to say to a young boy,' Mrs Winifred Oddicott always said when her grandson came in, breathless from pounding down the cliff path. 'You must say thank-you at the end of your lesson and then go, dear. He will not really want to be bothered with you, he is . . . well, a clever man, someone rather important. And old. Besides . . .'

'What? Besides what?'

'Nothing, James. Finish up all your beans.'

But later, to Deirdre Fount, she would say again that she did not quite like it.

'You never *know*, dear. You never know.'

'Oh, mother, what are you talking about? What do you never know? How suspicious you are, you see harm lurking everywhere.'

'Thank you, but I believe I have just *some* idea of what is right. I have lived longer than you, if I may say so, there are things I have learned. I know what is what. And it is a worry to me, for James is a growing boy, it is . . . it may not be *healthy*.'

Ashamed of her mother, irritated beyond bearing by such remarks and also much concerned, Deirdre Fount would leave the room, and refuse to listen to more. She would go and look at James, see the blond hairs that grew in a fine line over the knot of his neck and be inexplicably afraid.

Afterwards, if she spoke of it vaguely, Mrs Oddicott would then say, 'Oh, but he is such a good teacher, dear, so highly regarded. I believe his pupils come from a long distance away, so we are fortunate that he thinks it worthwhile to give lessons to James. We must make the best of things.'

And so, for weeks and months, the subject would be dropped.

'You are very foolish to go out, Bertram, there is a thick sea mist and you will be chilled to the bone. Surely in this weather you do not expect Mr Isepp to be there?'

Major Bertram Carpenter buttoned his greatcoat, searched about for his brown felt hat, his grey muffler and said nothing.

'Once you get a cold you find it so hard to get rid of. It will turn into bronchitis again and we will have all the trouble of last year. That is just why we went abroad, I thought, to set you up for the winter, but if you are determined to do foolhardy things, you will only have yourself to blame.'

Major Carpenter rolled up the *Daily Telegraph* and tucked it under his arm.

'Especially as the winter has scarcely begun. I think it is very rash and Mr Isepp will certainly have more sense than you.'

Major Carpenter walked to the door. 'I do not intend to be home for tea,' he said. And went out.

I do not mean to nag, she thought, wandering uneasily about the room, I have always despised wives who nag and I hear my own voice and am ashamed. It is so trying to be nagged, I do know that. Yet it *is* cold and there *is* a bad fog, he *will* be chilled. She could not bear to think of it all over again, the fever and the tossing and turning all night, the procession of doctors, medicine, linctus, pills, and above all, Major Carpenter's ill-temper. But he was a stubborn man, there was nothing she could do.

Over the whole of the bay and the Esplanade, lay the sea fog, and stretched its soft furred fingers down lanes and between houses, into the town. Looking at it through the windows, Mrs

Carpenter thought of the day ahead, a dull day with nothing to do, and only the winter beyond it. She was not often depressed.

If it were not for the fog, she would have gone shopping, called on Mrs Fount and Mrs Oddicott to buy some embroidery silks, had tea and cakes in Hoskins, visited Violet Prug. But she could not cope with the clammy air and the groping along, hands to railings, not even for so short a distance.

Instead, she took her embroidery down into the Red Lounge, for someone was sure to come and if it was one of the guests of whom Major Carpenter disapproved, well, he was out for the afternoon, he would not know.

The people of whom Major Carpenter disapproved were – almost all summer visitors, all conference members, the Jewish businessmen from Hampstead and engineering executives from the Midlands, solicitors and retired Diocesan Bishops, who came for Christmas and for three, or four or six weeks at a time, out of the season.

Mrs Flora Carpenter would excuse him, tell people that he was not a snob, could live and let live, but was old-fashioned, did not quite understand these people. She, who liked almost everybody, thought that it was a pity and felt a little guilty, tried to make amends as best she could. She would say 'Good morning', and 'Good night', offer a newspaper after she had done with it, or go out of her way to be helpful with information about the times of church services and the location of various hotel cloakrooms.

'Really,' she would tell her husband, 'when you make some effort and get to know them, why they are all so very nice!'

'They are not people I care to have to do with,' was the reply she would invariably receive.

In the Red Lounge today she found the very fat wife of a diamond merchant to whom Major Carpenter had been rude the previous evening. It was the least she could do, therefore, to strike up a conversation about the weather and, later, about the patterns for silk embroidery.

Major Bertram Carpenter coughed his way through the fog along the Esplanade towards the putting green and his meeting with Isepp. He met his friend Isepp every day at two. Isepp had no wife to contend with, only a subservient housekeeper, and he was an old man, almost eighty, so that Major Carpenter felt somewhat responsible. He had been uncertain about going on the cruise, for a long time, because of leaving Isepp.

Away to his left the fog horn sounded its low, low note. Major Carpenter pulled his muffler up, and thought of the West Indies. The dome shelter was empty, there was no Isepp yet. He unfolded the *Daily Telegraph* and sat until ten minutes to three, looking up every ten seconds and feeling the damp start to seep through his greatcoat. The shelter smelled of cold walls and dead cigarette butts. Isepp did not come.

An hour later, the fog had thinned, his way ahead was almost clear, but dank rain pattered through all the branches of trees and dripped on to his brown felt hat. Chestnut Avenue, in the suburb of clerks and junior solicitors and the keepers of chemist's shops, was the home of Isepp.

'Well,' said Major Carpenter at number fifty-eight, 'thank God I have no further to walk.'

The housekeeper was a thin woman with eyebrows that joined together over her nose, and a bloodless face. She held the front door close to her body, as though afraid he might somehow sneak past her through a crack, into the house.

'Look here, this is all very inconvenient, and what is the explanation? Isepp has no telephone, which is a barbarous thing, and insists upon living miles out on the very edge of the town – the bus does not even stop in the same road. It has always seemed to me a most unsatisfactory way of going on, and never more so than today, in such weather. But that is incidental, I am here in spite of the fog. Be so good as to tell him.'

'Mr Isepp cannot see you, Major, he . . .'

'He is not here? Well, I should have known this would be the way, that he would forget to look in his pocketbook and ascertain the date of our return from holiday. I have waited for over an hour, I may have caught a chill, the man is no longer reliable. Still, it has been a habit of ours for a good many years, we have always met at this time – so he has forgotten? But I do not need to stand here, none of this is of interest to you, there is . . .'

'Mr Isepp is very ill, I am just now waiting for the doctor to come again. That is why he did not keep his appointment, Major, and that is why you cannot see him.'

'Nonsense, of course I may see him. If he is ill, he will need a visitor, company makes all the difference to the bedridden. I take it that he *is* bedridden?'

'He has bronchial pneumonia, Major Carpenter, not an illness to be treated lightly.'

'Well, he is a strong fellow, he will get over it. As a young man, he told me, he suffered from some tropical fever for the best part of four years, but he survived, he has a good constitution. Do not dramatize trivialities.'

'He is an old man, eighty years old. And sick.'

'I will take your word for it, Madam, since you have nursed him and I have not. Though women know less than they claim about these affairs. But I do not see that his condition can be in any way worsened by my presence. I will not make him choke with laughter and so have a coughing fit, I will not raise his temperature by telling unsuitable stories. We will talk quietly of sane, everyday matters, have no fear.'

The houses of Chestnut Avenue were detached, though rather small, with wicker gates and fences leading to side gardens, and paintwork of maroon or green or black. Everything appeared to be separate and private, behind the fences or the holly hedge. Nothing was so.

'You had better come in,' said the housekeeper, 'to the hall, at least.' For Mrs Purdy was busying herself among the dustbins outside number fifty-six.

In the hall was an oak chest and a warming pan and a tinted picture of Caernarvon Castle. It smelled of boot-polish and mackintoshes and the curious, sour-sweet smell of the very ill.

'I was the one who found him here and got him to bed, I had all that responsibility. Who knows how long he had been lying in a delirium and everything all to sixes and sevens in the house, the budgerigars not even fed. I came and not a moment too soon but where was everyone else? If it had been left to others . . .'

'Do not accuse *me* of neglecting him, Madam, for three months I have been away travelling, quite out of touch, I did not return until Sunday last. Do not . . .'

'Neighbours, Major Carpenter, it was to neighbours that I referred. Those who live on the very doorstep and mind other people's business until such time as it might inconvenience them. *They* are the ones.'

'Yes, yes.' Major Carpenter made purposefully for the stairs. 'I will call you if anything is needed.'

'Wait, if you please, until I have ascertained whether he is fit and not sleeping or in a fever. Just allow me . . .'

Mrs Momus straightened her floral apron and prepared again to block his way. He resented her high-handed treatment, was not used to being so curtly dismissed and so he was prepared to stand his ground. An argument would have ensued. For eleven years he had known Isepp, and Mrs Momus had occupied this house during seven of them. For those seven years, she and Major Carpenter had loathed one another.

But in the event, there was no argument. From upstairs came the voice of Isepp, strained and delirious, and at the same time, the front door bell sounded, the doctor came.

'Now,' said Mrs Momus, removing her apron, 'now you *cannot* go upstairs, Major, you will have to wait in here.' She walked ahead of him into the sitting room, flung open the door. 'I will inform you,' she said, 'have no fear, I will bring down the doctor's verdict.'

Major Bertram Carpenter went into the sitting room and shut the door at once and sharply, in the housekeeper's face.

Chapter Three

WHATEVER Deirdre may say, thought Mrs Winifred Oddicott, there is something amiss. I cannot just put my finger on it, but I am uneasy. I must – investigate? Yes, that may be the word. I must do my duty, certainly, though it may turn out to be distasteful. But that is the way of things, women alone have to make their presence felt in this world, or they will very quickly go under. *They* are not able to cling and depend. I have been worried about this particular situation for some time, I realize that now.

It seemed to her that Deirdre Fount did not understand or even care. She is a naïve girl, thought Mrs Oddicott, an innocent with a veil drawn across her eyes. It is up to me to defend and protect her – both of them – they have been entrusted to my care, that is plain. I have been shown a little of the nastiness of human nature in order that I may save those close to me from it, and from themselves. To all things there is a purpose.

And so, on the Wednesday afternoon, half-day closing for the drapery shop, Mrs Oddicott ate her lunch and washed up her plate and did not follow her daughter into the sitting room, where the accounts waited to be done. Instead, she looked into her wardrobe and chose, with much care, a black coat and a maroon hat with feathers. 'Now I am just out for an hour, dear. Do not work too hard, do not give yourself a lot of trouble. If you have any queries, they can wait until I return. I should put my feet up if I were you, get some rest . . .'

'You are very concerned for my welfare all of a sudden. Why is this?'

'Oh, now what an unkind remark!' Mrs Winifred Oddicott wagged her forefinger. 'As if I am not always concerned, as if your welfare has not been the guiding consideration of my life! You work hard and I think you enjoy your free afternoon.'

'Thank you. But I intend to make use of it for the accounts. If I do not do them, who else will?'

'Well, please yourself then. I shall not be so very long away.'

Mrs Oddicott turned her back. Deirdre Fount turned her back. There was a silence. But Mrs Oddicott did not go at once.

'I do not like to say this . . .' she began.

'Then why must you?'

'Yes, *there* it is, that is precisely what I am meaning! It is becoming very tiresome, very irritating, Deirdre, this sharp way of talking, into which you have just recently fallen. The pertness and curtness of tone. It is unlike you, something must be wrong.'

'I daresay it is the onset of another winter.' Deirdre Fount opened the Petty Cash book and prepared to add up a column of figures, for she did not want to have this conversation with her mother.

'I suppose that you may be anaemic.'

'Nonsense.'

'Oh, it is a common complaint in our family, Deirdre, and nothing to be ashamed of. It accounts for so much, you . . .'

'There is nothing wrong with my blood. It is thick and rich and I have plenty of it.'

'Now you are being ridiculous.'

'I am sorry. I am trying to settle down to my work.'

'Very well, I shall say no more. I had to mention it, that is all. I *am* your mother.'

'What time are you planning to return?'

Mrs Winifred Oddicott stiffened. But Deirdre Fount, growing afraid of herself and feeling that she must draw back now, if they were to have any peace in their daily life, looked round in a conciliatory way at her mother.

'I am not asking where you are going, or what is your business. But I will put on a kettle for you, if you give me an approximate time. That is all.'

Mrs Oddicott pulled her black gloves more tightly on to her wrists. I have a good daughter after all, she thought, she is an amiable girl, on the whole, and perhaps there is nothing wrong with her except that it is the end of November and she dreads the coughs and sinus trouble she will suffer as the winter progresses. She needs my protection and support, needs to feel forgiven after she has been a little sharp with me. Life has been a disappointment to her, in many ways, although it was partly her own fault for being so headstrong. But now she has me, she is fortunate and settled. And so she said, 'About four. I hope I shall not be later than four.' She put up a hand to pat the maroon feathers, and left.

Deirdre Fount was not easy in her mind. Where is she going, she asked, and what business of mine is she meddling in? For she had not liked the evasive, secret look on her mother's face. Something was wrong.

The fire spluttered and the clock chimed a quarter to three, in the chintzy sitting room, and Mrs Deirdre Fount tackled the Petty Cash, for if she did not, she would get up and wander about the house, and think dissatisfied thoughts about James and Aubrey, about the past and the future and the dull present. Though perhaps, after all, her mother might be right about the anaemia, perhaps it was as simple as that. The idea that she might be able to take a short course of some sort of tonic tablets and by these means alone lay all her ghosts and satisfy her irritations, filled her with hope. If that is true, she thought, then I shall be grateful to my mother, though I do not like her to be always right.

She applied herself to the accounting.

Half an hour later, climbing the long hill, Mrs Winifred Oddicott began to have doubts and indeed, almost changed her mind and her direction. What if he should insult, or even attack her, what if he should suspect the reasons for her visit? What if she should discover some terrible truth? Though she had no idea of what that truth might be, only saw that she would never be able to cope with it. And she was a woman long accustomed to being praised for her powers of coping. Perhaps she had taken too much upon herself.

But in the end, she continued on up the hill. It is not for me, after all, she said, it is for the sake of my grandson, a boy of only eleven. She hated to waste anything, too, even a journey, and she was extremely *curious*.

I am on my way, she said, I shall get to the bottom of this, sum up the situation for myself and ferret out the truth. It may be perfectly innocent, all above board, but it has seemed very odd to me for a long time, *very* odd.

From the bay, the fog horn began again to sound its low, low note.

Major Carpenter had never approved of Isepp's housekeeper, Mrs Momus, nor did he approve his choice of doctor.

'You surround yourself with unsuitable, even objectionable people,' he had said one day, in the dome shelter, 'they prey upon your easy nature. You should not be content with anything but the best, where your health and welfare are concerned.'

But Isepp had waved his hand, and fumbled for one of his sticks which had slipped from the bench to the floor and would not hear a word spoken against either of them, the man or the woman. That was an irritating trait in Isepp, that he would never hear words spoken against anyone, no matter that they were the truth. Major Carpenter suspected that his friend was faint-hearted, a little soft at the centre.

'It is because he cannot stand up for himself,' he told Mrs Flora Carpenter, 'he has no courage for a fight. It is the easiest way out, to put up with inefficiency and laziness and second-rate service. No wonder I stick to Isepp, he needs someone of my sort to prop him up, keep him going. He would give in to anyone at all, given half a chance.'

Major Carpenter saw himself as being obliged to carry Isepp permanently under his wing. And so, he was glad to be faced, now, with this doctor of whom he had long disapproved. The man spoke in a jolly, convivial tone, and lit a cigarette.

'That is a very unhealthy habit,' said Major Bertram Carpenter. 'I am surprised you do not know it, as a medical man, surprised you do not feel called upon to set an example.'

'Ah,' said the doctor, the lapels of whose blue suit were vaguely greasy, 'the spirit is willing, but we all know about the flesh! It has to be a case of do as I say, not as I do, eh? Yes, my goodness.' And ash from the cigarette dropped on to Isepp's Indian carpet.

'I am sending him off to hospital, Major. Yes. Best thing all round, best place for him. We'll have them give him a good overhaul.'

'Hospital? Do you always hospitalize the sufferers from colds and coughs, in these days of the Welfare State? I am a bronchitic and I have a good deal to put up with in the winter months, but you do not hear me complaining, and nobody has ever tried to hospitalize me.'

'He is eighty, you know, eighty. There is rather more to it than a cold, you know, at his age.'

'*What more?*' Major Carpenter took a step forward, nearer to the fat doctor, and peered into his face. The doctor retreated. 'Do not hide behind your medical jargon, let us have this out in the open. *What more?*'

'Good gracious, good gracious! There is no need to start getting alarmed, Major, no need to think of something nasty in the woodshed and so forth. Nothing for you to worry about at all, no need for panic, because I mention hospital. Just a touch of congestion, nothing antibiotics cannot get rid of in a very short time, oh, no. Soon have him out of there, back on his feet. What feet he has, anyhow – what feet he has!'

'Either my friend is seriously ill,' said Major Carpenter, in a loud and distinct voice, 'or he is not.'

'Have him looked over, that's the idea. It never did any harm, especially not at his age. But there's nothing to worry about, I told the good lady as much. No, indeed.'

And the fat doctor took himself off, smoking the last of his cigarette, down the foggy suburban path.

Major Bertram Carpenter sat among the moquette chairs and the models of sailing ships, and made up his mind to speak to Isepp. He will listen to me, for that man will not do at all, he has no manner, no presence. I would not trust him.

'I would not trust him,' he said aloud to the housekeeper, Mrs Momus.

'Mr Isepp is seriously ill, he is to be taken to hospital. Now perhaps you will understand that I was right to bar the way to visitors. An ambulance will come.'

'It seems a great deal of fuss and nonsense to me, Madam. What can be done in a hospital that cannot be done here? There is more to this than meets the eye, I can tell you, that doctor conceals some secret behind his bland manner. He thought I was a half-wit, that much was clear. Or else he wants to get out of work and responsibility; pass the buck on to the hospital.'

Mrs Momus stood by the sitting-room door, anxious for Major Carpenter to be gone so that the full drama of the ambulance might be savoured alone.

'I have every confidence,' she said stiffly, 'every confidence . . .'

'I daresay that is typical.' Major Bertram Carpenter wound his muffler with care about his thin neck. 'I daresay that attitude is only to be expected. I shall visit Isepp in hospital. It may be a good deal easier to gain admittance there, and talk to him undisturbed. Good morning to you.'

Though he had half thought of waiting until the ambulance should arrive and asking to be carried as far as the Prince of Wales Hotel. But the housekeeper might also want to be there. And also, as had occurred to him during his conversation with the doctor, you could not be too careful. Isepp might have some infectious disease, about which mention was not being made. Nothing had been stated, but everything had been implied, the words of the doctor now seemed, as Major Carpenter looked back over them, to be dark with lurking threats. It was a bad show that Isepp had to be left to the mercies of an ambulance attendant and the objectionable housekeeper but it was unwise to take risks, nevertheless.

Waiting for the bus, in the dripping fog, Major Carpenter thought that his wife might conceivably have been right, and he might catch a cold. The bus came. But it is all in the service of an old friend, he told himself, at times risks *have* to be taken. He was much comforted by this, believing that, as his journey had been undertaken entirely out of charitable, unselfish motives, his reward would be *not* to catch cold.

'Come on, pay up, old soldier,' said the bus conductor, dangling from the overhead rail by one arm like a monkey. Major Carpenter set his face into an expression of displeasure, and the bus took him slowly back towards the Prince of Wales Hotel.

She had expected to hear music coming from the house, and so she had pressed very hard upon the doorbell. But there was silence, except for, all around her outside, the sound of the wind. It is a very weird place, thought Mrs Winifred Oddicott, I would not care to live up here, with my garden sloping down to the very edge of that dangerous cliff and not a neighbour in sight until the Priory. He lives quite alone, he does not even have a housekeeper, which makes everything seem even more untoward. He must be a man of very peculiar disposition. And her nerve, which had failed her again and again on the way, was retrieved as she thought of this man Porlock, alone in such a house with her young grandson, and of the dark, lonely cliff path down which the boy had to walk, after his music lesson.

Mrs Oddicott pressed the doorbell again and wondered if Deirdre would take to heart what she had said about the anaemia. As a girl, she had always accepted good advice and acted upon it, her mother had been able to tell her what was best for her. But just now, she was not herself, she was behaving in an irritating and also an absent-minded way. For instance, only that morning, Mrs Christie had come in for some crochet cotton and had naturally expected Deirdre to know what colour and weight were required, since it was to complete the pattern that they had sold to her the week before. It was their duty to remember such things, that was why they kept a shop, to give service of that kind. Customers in Westbourne expected these details about size of needle and colour of thread, make of wool and number of ounces, to be remembered by Mrs Fount and Mrs Oddicott, for it saved them the trouble of remembering themselves, it made them feel significant and cared for. And Deirdre was always most conscientious, the customers came to rely upon her. Yet there she had stood, foolish and flustered, over the tray of crochet cottons, and said, 'I am sorry, but I have quite forgotten which pattern it was, and what kind you now require. We have so very many customers, you will have to go back home and find out the details.'

Mrs Christie had stared and looked much offended, it had all been most embarrassing. Mrs Oddicott had sent Deirdre off into the back stockroom, to check on the rolls of wide tapestry canvas, and under cover of her absence, had whispered across to Mrs Christie that Deirdre was not quite herself just at the moment, that she was a little run-down and over-tired. Mrs

Christie had been very kind, and gone away at once to find out about the crochet cotton. But afterwards, Deirdre Fount had only shrugged and said that it was not their business to do other people's thinking for them. Mrs Oddicott had tried very hard to keep her temper.

Well, if it is all because of this worry over James, about which she will not confide in me, Mrs Oddicott thought now, then I am here to set her mind at rest. But not for the first time, she wished that James Fount had been born a girl, for she knew how to cope with the problems of growing girls, and the dangers that beset them were only too familiar to her. Nor did girls at all need the presence of a father. Boys seemed to live to some extent in a world apart, their needs were unusual and at times Mrs Winifred Oddicott found it hard to assess them. Although James was a very quiet, well-mannered boy, and full of respect, there was no problem there.

If Deirdre is obstinate and refuses to see a doctor, thought Mrs Oddicott, then I shall have to take it upon myself to call him in. She will not be able to back out of submitting to a thorough examination when he calls at the house and stands there waiting, and she knows full well that his time is precious. Well, she should be very grateful, it is a great blessing that she has me to look after her, and James, for she would never, never cope alone, she has not the least idea. For Mrs Oddicott remembered that her daughter had tried, and quickly failed, to cope with pregnancy and childbirth and the needs of a small baby, alone, and when she had called upon her mother in desperation, she had gone only too willingly, to encourage and advise, comfort and console, to take charge.

Mrs Oddicott listened to the sea, as it turned restlessly over upon itself, time after time. I am quite alone here, she thought suddenly. I have told nobody where I have come. I could be accosted and attacked by anyone on this path, or standing outside this house, and it would be a very long time before I was found. The previous summer two schoolgirls had been followed up here and raped, one after the other, in the long dry grass, by a man in a blue shirt. Thinking of it, Mrs Winifred Oddicott trembled with apprehension and distaste.

It was very cold on the doorstep, and the man was clearly not at home, she had been here quite long enough. She would make her way back down the cliff path, holding her umbrella like a bayonet before her. She turned. The front door opened.

Isepp was a bad colour. Major Bertram Carpenter stood beside the iron-framed hospital bed and did not know what to do with his hands, for he had never given in to the slovenly habit of hiding them in his pockets. Isepp was the colour of sour porridge and his skin had a faint bloom of sweat. His breathing sounded nasty.

'His breathing sounds nasty,' said Major Carpenter to the hare-lipped nurse.

'You may not stay more than a moment, he isn't to be disturbed.' And she rammed the breathing mask more firmly on to Isepp's face.

Isepp lay with his eyes closed.

Major Carpenter had not been able to rest at the hotel, he had eaten a good tea and then come at once to the hospital. They had reassured him on the question of infection, but with curious, half-laughing expressions on their faces. He had come into the small room and said, 'Well now, here we are and what's all this?' in a cheerful voice. But Isepp had seemed not to hear him.

'Yes, you get your bit of rest, don't you take any notice of me. Have you better in no time, with some rest,' said Major Carpenter.

Isepp's eyelids had twitched.

'Try and keep a cheerful face on things, that is always the best. I shall be in and out, keeping an eye on you, you can rely on me.'

Isepp had lain very still under the breathing mask. After that, there was nothing more to say. At first, Major Carpenter had sat on the chair beside the bed, his hands dangling awkwardly from his knees. His yellow muffler had unwound itself, and fallen forward on to Isepp's pillow.

The skin on top of Isepp's head was flaking slightly, like the scurf-cap on the head of a baby. Major Carpenter had stared at it and felt most uncomfortable, alone with the unconscious man. He had not known where to look.

A doctor had come in, and then a nurse and another doctor, and they had all ignored Major Carpenter, and he had stared out of the window at the fog, while they busied themselves about Isepp. After ten minutes, he stood up, and then hesitated, in case the movement should wake his friend, and there would be something to say after all, a point to the visit. Isepp did not move. Major Bertram Carpenter wound his muffler and put on his gloves and wondered whether he should pat his friend on the shoulder, as a gesture of reassurance. As a young soldier in Malaya, he had watched men die and they had all been grateful for the touch of a man. But Isepp was not dying, and so he drew himself up, and said, 'Well, Isepp. Well ...' and left the room quickly.

In the beige corridor, he met a doctor.

'You had better leave your name and address at the reception desk,' the man had said.

'My address?'

'Aren't you the next-of-kin?'

'He has no kin, sir, no family living. I am his friend.'

'Then that will do. Leave your address at the desk.'

'Why should that be necessary? Isepp knows where you can contact me, if he feels like a visit. You have only to ask him.'

'He may not be ...'

'No, I agree about that, he won't answer you just now. He looks in poor shape, to me.'

'Indeed ...'

'Of course, you will get going with your drugs and so on, have him back to normal in no time. That is what I have been given to understand.'

'By whom?'

'By his own doctor, sir, his general practitioner, who else?'

The doctor pursed his mouth but said nothing. His hands were stuffed into the pockets of his trousers, under cover of the white coat.

'He'll be sitting up and taking notice before long,' Major Carpenter told him, 'there is a lot of fight in Isepp, a lot of stamina. I have known him for many years.'

The doctor, a man of forty-seven with soured hopes and contempt for the ignorance of the layman, looked at Major Bertram

Carpenter and saw that it was not quite too late to tell him the probable truth. But it was tedious, it was a nuisance, the man would never understand and neither patient nor doctor would profit by it. And so he said, hastily, 'I daresay you are right, but you had better leave your address to be on the safe side. You could say that it was a mere formality.' He turned away through the doors into Isepp's room.

Now there is a straightforward, sensible man, thought Major Carpenter, a man who does not waste words, nor spread unnecessary gloom, not one of your secretive medicos. He has said, I daresay you are right.

Major Carpenter walked with a firm tread along the hospital corridors, keeping his eyes steadily ahead of him, for fear of catching sight of some unpleasantness through a half-open door.

At the reception desk, he asked for a taxi to be called, and gave his name and address.

'But it is most unlikely that you will need it,' he told the supercilious girl, 'I have that on medical authority. Most unlikely. Isepp will battle through.'

The taxi was a very long time in coming.

'Madam?'

He wore a grey apron, over a stiff white shirt, and in his left hand he carried a butcher's cleaver. Mrs Winifred Oddicott stepped back in some alarm.

'Oh! Good afternoon. I was quite sure that you were not at home, I had given up ringing the bell and was going away. You are Mr Porlock, of course, Mr Ralph Porlock?'

'Of course.'

'I hope I am not intruding, not disturbing you at ...'

Mrs Oddicott looked vaguely at the cleaver and dared not suggest at what she might have disturbed him.

'Have we met before, Madam? I do not recall ...'

'Of course, how foolish of me! No, we have not met, although I do feel that I know you, I have heard such a great deal about you, and not only from James. Your reputation is such a good one, we knew of you even before you came to Westbourne. My name is Oddicott, Mrs Winifred Oddicott, and my grandson is your pupil. Fount – James Fount. Now, if you could spare me a few moments of your time, it would be so kind, such a comfort for me to talk about James with you. It would set my mind at rest. If you are not too busy . . .'

'Is there something wrong with James?'

'Wrong? Oh, you mean is he ill? Well, how kind of you to enquire – no, no, he is quite well, he has always been a strong child on the whole, at least since the removal of his tonsils and adenoids, which caused so much trouble in the winter – you cannot imagine – when he was a little boy. He did not *grow*, you see, would not eat a thing, we were very, very worried about him. Oh, and not just his mother and I, the doctors were most worried, they could not see how . . . but then after the operation, he simply never looked back. He was seven at the time.'

'Indeed?'

Mrs Oddicott, tired of the man's disdainful expression and of the cold wind blowing about her, as she stood upon the doorstep, said firmly, 'But I see that it is not a convenient time for you, after all. Perhaps I may call again and discuss the matter?'

'What matter is this?'

'Really, Mr Porlock, you cannot expect me to go into details and make the proper enquiries, while standing here on the step.'

'Then you had better come inside.'

Mrs Oddicott hesitated. He was a very peculiar man, as she had long suspected, and he appeared to be quite alone in the house. Perhaps she had been foolish to come, perhaps it would not be wise . . .

But the man had walked away from her across a dark hall and through an arch, into the room ahead, and so Mrs Oddicott could do nothing but follow him, though she left the front door wide open behind her, as some sort of a precaution.

Mr Porlock had set the butcher's cleaver down on top of a music stool, and stood beside the windows, waiting for her to begin. Outside, there was only the fog.

'Well, now,' said Mrs Winifred Oddicott, 'I do not mean to keep you very long.'

'No?'

'I am quite aware that you are a very busy man, you have such a lot of pupils and so on, we have heard all about you. I said to my daughter Deirdre, only the other day – and of course,

I have said it to others, many times before – I said that James is a very lucky boy, he simply does not realize, to have Mr Porlock for his music lessons. One of the best flute teachers in the country, so I have heard, even though I do not really understand about these matters. Of course, I realize that you are now more or less retired, and only take on very special pupils, and of course, you do not find a boy like James every day, I am sure, so I hope that the matter is not entirely one-sided.'

'It was about James Fount that you wish to talk to me?'

'Yes. Or rather . . .'

'Have you something to *tell* me?'

In fact, Mrs Oddicott did not know. For now she was here, in this most extraordinary room, among so many unusual objects, and with the butcher's cleaver still in evidence, she realized that she had nothing to say, her plans had been of the vaguest. She could not begin to voice all her doubts and suspicions, or to ask the questions she had uppermost in her mind, about the time James spent here after his flute lessons were over, for the man was not to be chatted to in a general, friendly way, there was nothing in his manner that encouraged her, made her feel at ease. Clearly, he would never respond to hints or a tactful steering of the conversation. Well, thought Mrs Oddicott, he is a man, and it is all that can be expected, there is no softening, civilizing influence in this house, that is plain. But I should not have come, he is staring at me so rudely, making me feel uncomfortable and foolish.

'James is a very *sensitive* boy,' she said, in the end.

Mr Porlock said nothing. He had not asked her to sit down, and remained standing himself. She did not quite know how to manage her handbag, gloves and umbrella, and also, felt even more at a disadvantage when standing up to talk, and so she perched on the very edge of a straight-backed cane chair.

'What was I about to say? Oh, yes! He is sensitive and because of that, of course, he is also very shy and reserved, almost a timid boy, you might say, though there is never anything foolish in his manner, we have brought him up to speak well in front of adults. But he has been protected, you see, perhaps far more than the usual run of boys, and he does not see danger lying in wait for him because he has never had to face any kind of danger. I have seen to that, for there is plenty of unpleasantness and misery to be witnessed when he is an adult, I do not want him to have a frightened, oppressed childhood. James does not understand that other people are perhaps ...' Mrs Oddicott stopped, uncertain how to phrase her anxieties. The man still said nothing, gave her no help.

'And he is artistic, as you know. He does love his music.'

Mrs Oddicott thought it extremely rude of Mr Ralph Porlock to make absolutely no reply, not so much as a murmur of agreement. It was almost as though he stood silent because he did *not* agree, and she was considerably offended. He has been brought up to think of himself as someone extraordinary, she decided, someone to whom everybody looks up and for whom the ordinary rules of polite behaviour do not apply. But I am not impressed and I am not intimidated by such rudeness. Mr Porlock stood by the long window, looking out, and his hands rested lightly on an armillary sphere, the bright, sharp arrow of which pointed in Mrs Oddicott's direction.

'Well, Mr Porlock, the fact of the whole matter is that I am very worried about James, and I knew that it could not go on, that I should have to come and speak to you. I thought that you would be able to set my mind at rest, or to advise me.'

'His musical progress is more than satisfactory.'

'Oh, why yes, naturally! That goes without saying, I hope.'

'It does?'

'Well, he is a clever boy, he takes after my side of the family in his being sensitive and artistic, we have all been prone to a keen appreciation of culture, the finer side of life. Though I must confess that I am very practical, it is my daughter who is rather a dreamer. And James works so very hard at his music, nothing is too much, and he is never allowed to skip his practice time. But then, he never wants to, I do not have to stand over him with a stop-watch, Mr Porlock.'

'I am relieved to hear it.'

'Sometimes, indeed, I wonder if he plays his flute for too long, he will be upstairs for hours and hours, and I do not think it is always good for him, when he should be getting out in the fresh air, or doing his other school-work. I . . .'

'Madam, I do not yet know why you have come to see me. I

am, as you have said, a busy man, I would be grateful if you would now speak out plainly.'

Mrs Oddicott flushed. She could not now say anything about the time he and the boy spent here together, could not ask what they talked about, nor say that she did not think it altogether suitable. James was totally uncommunicative, and she herself was alarmed, even more so now that she had met the rude Mr Ralph Porlock and seen what a bad influence he must be upon James. But none of it could be spoken, and so she had to say quickly, 'I do not, I must confess to you, at all like the idea of James's returning home alone, down that cliff path. Especially in the dark, in winter. *That* is really why I have had to come here to see you. It is not safe, Mr Porlock, and you must see why it is not safe.'

'Why do you not come and collect him, then, if you are so alarmed?'

'I have a business to run, Mr Porlock, I am not free to come and go just as I please.'

'The boy is eleven years old. He has been returning down that cliff path alone, in the dark and in winter, for some years. There has been no hint of alarm before this. I was not aware of it. No other parent has complained. James Fount is perfectly sensible, and as safe down the cliff path as anywhere in this town at night. The path is broad and well set back from the grass that leads to the cliff edge. He would be in no danger of falling.'

'Oh, I do not think that he might *fall*, it is not of falling that I am afraid. James is quite careful and steady on his feet, and the path itself is in no way dangerous. No, indeed.'

'Then what are you suggesting?'

Mrs Oddicott was shocked that the man should not have the wit to grasp at once any implications behind her words, and the tact to excuse her from stating them.

'Madam,' he said now, 'the world is full of all manner of dangers, the boy is of an age when all manner of unpleasant things might happen to him. These things are to be faced. You say that you have sheltered and protected your grandson. Let me tell you now that you are thereby doing him a grave disservice, you are failing to equip him realistically for his adult life. In fact, I think your grandson has a clear head and a shrewd sense of what goes on in the world about him. He may not suffer as a result of all this shielding. And if the cliff path were not safe, if several boys and girls of various ages were in any danger there, do you suppose that I should allow them to descend it?'

'Things have happened there, girls have been – have been set upon. Accosted.'

'Once, yes. In the middle of a summer afternoon.'

'Nobody knows what may be the danger, then, on a dark winter's evening.'

'Tush, Madam. No more than the danger outside your own house.'

'I do not . . .'

'Mrs Oddicott, when I took on the boy James as my pupil, I had an interview with his mother. She, presumably, saw the cliff path for herself at that time – when your grandson was considerably younger – and considered the situation, but was happy with it.'

'My daughter does not see danger, she is something of an innocent. She . . .'

'And now, if there is nothing more you have to ask me . . .?'

Mrs Oddicott was obliged to stand up, and follow him out of the room, towards the front door.

'You will excuse me, I am sure, but I have a great deal to do. I am cutting up a hare.'

Mrs Oddicott faced the man Porlock, holding herself very straight.

'I will only hope for your sake that none of these young children comes to grief – of *any* kind – one winter's night. I felt that it was my duty to speak of it, and I am only sorry that I have had such a poor reception.'

And she walked away down the path, still red about the neck with anger. Ralph Porlock, seeing the humour of it, smiled to himself because as he got older, he found the quest for the risible more and more fully rewarded. But, as he returned with his cleaver, to the carcass of the hare, he saw that it was not, after all, so very amusing, because there was the boy James Fount, stifled, possessed, over-protected.

*

Mrs Winifred Oddicott breathed hard as she walked very quickly down the cliff path, for she was filled with resentment at having been made to look and feel so foolish. He should not be allowed to teach young children, she thought, those whose minds are not yet moulded and who may so easily be influenced. He is ill-mannered and eccentric and peculiar. I will talk to Deirdre about it all, and we must decide whether the risk of his affecting James is worth running, just because of the boy's music. Deirdre must be made to understand.

The root of the matter was, she decided, that Mr Ralph Porlock had no respect for women, he did not know how to address them. James was brought up to treat women chivalrously, for such things were too little regarded these days, and they were most important. This is a courteous and respectful town, Mrs Oddicott thought, we do not want people of that boorish kind among us, whatever their reputation.

For she had been brought up to believe that the higher a man advanced up the ladder of worldly success, the greater his position and wealth and reputation, then the more reason he had to be humble and well-mannered and respectful to women. Royalty, she knew, had the very best manners of all.

Mrs Winifred Oddicott marched on, up the garden path between the stiff, standard roses, no longer feeling foolish and belittled, only determined. The front door key was already to hand.

'Deirdre,' she said at once, 'I hope you have the kettle boiling and the accounts done, for this matter will not wait. I shall ask you to listen carefully, and it is to be discussed and settled between us at once. I have endured a great deal of unpleasantness this afternoon, let us see that it is not all in vain.'

Deirdre Fount did not reply. The house was empty.

Chapter Four

'BERTRAM, dear, the gentleman spoke to you. He said good evening.'

'I am well aware of it.'

'You did not reply.'

'I did not.'

Major Carpenter pulled his roast beef impatiently about on his plate.

'I do not know what butcher they patronize, I am sure, but this is deplorable meat, somebody should tell them, something ought to be done. I shall have to have a word with Plumb. The fellow should be struck off their list of suppliers.'

'I am sure he is wondering why you ignored him, Bertram. I do wish you would be a little more ...'

'What? More what?'

'Well ...'

'What, Flora? Come along, speak out, say what you have to say no matter how unpleasant.'

'I was only meaning, more *polite*. It does no harm.'

'I do not choose to hobnob with every Tom, Dick and Harry who stays in this hotel, that is not why I pay to live here. And if you must know, I do not like the look of that fellow. I daresay he is some kind of salesman.'

'He cannot help that, Bertram.'

'Of course he can help it, what nonsense you talk, Flora! And how like a woman to make a remark of that kind. A man can always help what he *does*, it is a result of his own free choice. Not like the colour of his hair and eyes. And what he does influences the kind of man he is.'

'But he may not be a salesman, after all.'

'He is quite sure to be. I know a salesman when I see one, it is something about their eyes. They have shifty eyes. And hands.

Yes, come to think of it, hands too. They cannot seem to keep their hands still for five seconds.'

Mrs Flora Carpenter bowed her head and did not argue further. She had grown accustomed to her husband's prejudices and did not hold them against him. She glanced at the man in question, who was now seated at a table by himself, in the far corner of the red and gold dining room, and she saw that he did have rather weak, and even shifty eyes, her husband had been quite right. The line of his jaw was very definite, too. Mrs Carpenter looked away again, and as she did so, caught the eye of the Jewish businessman's wife from Hampstead. Across the tables, the two women bowed. Major Carpenter glowered at his wife.

'Ah, now I will tell you what struck me today, Bertram,' she said quickly. For in another moment he would be making remarks about *those* people and his voice carried, he did not always realize, and it was often most embarrassing. 'Our dinner party.'

Major Carpenter pushed three quarters of the roast beef over to one side of his plate.

'There will not be any meat ordered, I can tell you, not on that occasion. Much better stick to fish, turbot, probably, you know where you are with fish, it seems to me.'

'Yes, dear, I am quite sure you're right. No, it occurred to me that if we are to invite Mrs Deirdre Fount – we *are* inviting Mrs Fount?'

'Of course we are, I thought you had seen to all that long ago.'

'Then should we not, out of common courtesy, also invite her mother, Mrs Oddicott?'

'Why?'

'Well, because they live together and she is her mother, dear.'

'I do not like this Westbourne habit of treating mothers and daughters, sisters and brothers, even women and their companions, as though they were natural pairs, inseparable like husband and wife. *That* is the only couple to be automatically invited, so far as etiquette is concerned.'

'Yes, Bertram, it is only that I should not like to offend anyone, and Mrs Oddicott is rather a touchy person, she might be a little upset.'

'Mrs Oddicott is monstrous, I will not have her piping and

fluting away at my dinner table. Let the daughter come alone, stand on her own two feet for once in a way.'

Mrs Carpenter sighed. She was, in fact, relieved.

'You have set my mind at rest, Bertram, I am quite content. I only thought it best to ask.'

Major Carpenter grunted and turned his attention to the waiter.

'Now look here, I cannot think what this hotel is coming to, your standards have reached rock bottom. Take this dish of meat back into your kitchen and tell your chef that I have never tasted worse, it is like string, like shoe leather – like *tent canvas,*' he said triumphantly. 'And tell the manager, that fellow Plumb, that I have no intention of paying for it.'

Mrs Flora Carpenter closed her eyes. When she opened them again, the waiter had gone and her husband was vigorously buttering a piece of melba toast. She glanced across the room again, at the man who sat alone. He wore a pin-striped suit and his tie gave off a faint sheen when it caught the light of the great chandelier.

'I think you may be right,' she said to her husband, for it would humour him, 'I think he may well be some kind of salesman.'

Mrs Deirdre Fount took the towel away from in front of her eyes. But the smarting had not been relieved, and tears still coursed down her cheeks. Her mother walked in from the dining room. As a mark of her displeasure, she had not removed her feathered hat, but wore it with her floral apron and a pursed mouth, to cook the evening meal.

'I have told you before, Deirdre, I cannot think how many times,' she said, glancing at her daughter, 'that if you chop them under water, running water, there is no odour and therefore, your eyes cannot be affected. I have no sympathy with you.'

Deirdre Fount would have said, the last time I tried to chop them under running water an onion shot from my hand and I cut myself quite badly, except that there was no point in making even such a simple remark, for there would only be silence, or some sharp reply. She pushed her face into the towel again and scrubbed at her eyelids.

At the sink, Mrs Winifred Oddicott washed liver and dried it and dipped it into seasoned flour and laid it into the greased frying pan.

'I take it that you have given in,' she said curtly, 'that because of the effect of the onions, you can do nothing more to help me. I had better finish chopping them myself.'

'There is no need.'

Deirdre Fount sat down at the kitchen table again and began, at arm's length, to finish the vegetables. Perhaps there would at least be silence. But Mrs Oddicott had by no means finished with the matter in hand.

'It would not have been so bad,' she said, therefore, 'if you had been doing something useful. Perhaps if you had done something I have often expected of you. I know you only have one free afternoon in the week, you are often at pains to tell me so...'

There was a pause, but Deirdre Fount did not take her up on it, and so Mrs Oddicott was forced to continue.

'I mean, of course, if you had gone to school to meet James. It would give him such pleasure, once in a while, Deirdre.'

Deirdre Fount stabbed at the glaucous onion flesh with her knife. Why is it that I can have nothing to myself, she thought, no idea, no little private argument, why is it that she sees into me so unfailingly? Am I so shallow and transparent?

But she only said, aloud, 'James is too old to be met from school.'

'Nonsense. I do not mean that you are to hold his hand going down the avenue, as though he were five years old again. But he would appreciate a show of interest and some company, now and then. Children think about these things, Deirdre, and he knows that you are free at four o'clock on a Wednesday, and yet you still leave him to walk home alone.'

'He has friends.'

'You are his mother! He would like to have the relationship publicly witnessed from time to time, it would make him feel happy and secure.'

'You have no idea, you are talking rubbish. James is not a child, he is a boy of eleven and a half, he lives his own independent life and he would be ashamed of having his mother wait for him at the school gates. Public display is what the young never want.'

For Deirdre Fount remembered the terrible sports days and open days and school concerts, when her mother would bear down upon everyone, keeping hold of her daughter's hand, patting her on the shoulder. She used to ask prying questions of teachers and pupils, and wear appalling hats. The memory of those afternoons was acutely painful. And it came back now because that afternoon, she herself had wanted very much to go and meet her son James from school, it had been with that idea in her mind that she had abandoned the accounts and gone out of the house. She wanted to walk with him down the avenue and have him tell her interesting things about his day, and Westbourne should see them together and say, 'There is Mrs Deirdre Fount and her growing son. How well they look together!' For she had realized that she did not know the boy at all, had never known him, he was a stranger to her and she needed to be reassured of their relationship. He was moving away, already he was eleven, there seemed to be so little time.

Half way to the school, she had stopped, and remembered the humiliation to which Mrs Oddicott had subjected her often and often, at the school gates. She could not go. She was afraid of James, of his distaste and disapproval and rejection, afraid of his cold, clear, unfriendly stare. She had walked away from Westbourne Priors School.

Mrs Winifred Oddicott was determined to know where Deirdre Fount had been, she had asked and hinted and taken offence for information which had not been given to her. The sense of hidden matters lay uneasily between them. Deirdre Fount had not returned home until seven o'clock, by which time James was home and fed, and in the middle of his preparation, and outside, it was quite dark, although the fog had cleared. Mrs Oddicott was not merely annoyed, but also anxious.

'Good heavens, mother, I am a grown woman, I am nearly forty years of age, I am answerable only to myself. Why should I not walk out of this house at any time I like, and go wherever I choose, without consulting anyone?'

'To begin with, because anything might have happened to

you, and I was not to know. That is all. Do not feel answerable to *me*, Deirdre, I am only your mother. But I am entitled to some consideration, I think. You are not quite a law unto yourself, so long as you live with us in this house.'

Deirdre Fount was silent.

'Whatever was I supposed to think? Finding an empty house, after I had left you doing the accounts quietly by the fire and talking of making a pot of tea on my return. You had not made any mention of plans for going out.'

'I had made no plans, I decided on the spur of the moment.'

'But that is not the way we ever behave, as a family. If there had been some kind of an accident, if you had been taken suddenly ill, and were lying in some hospital, waiting for me to come to you, if *that* had been the case, you would have been in a sorry state, had I come home and made myself tea and sat down for the evening, thought nothing of you, made no enquiries, perhaps even gone to bed ...'

'Oh, of course, if I had not come home at a reasonable time you would have been anxious. But it was only seven o'clock, let us please remember that, mother.'

'I returned myself in a state of some distress, I had spent a most unpleasant, even alarming afternoon and I needed to discuss it with you at once, I needed your reassurance and approval, and then we would have come to a decision. But you were not here.'

'Now we are coming to the heart of the matter. You are resentful that I was out when you wanted to relieve yourself of some worry or other.'

'I would have you remember that it was on *your* behalf that I went at all.'

'I did not know that. Where *did* you go?'

'You expect to be told that straight away, you wish to know my affairs ...'

'But you have just said that it was on my behalf.'

'Deirdre, you go out of your way to upset me, I cannot think what has got into you, as I mentioned earlier. You are unlike yourself.'

'Then I am not in the least interested in where you have been or what you have done. I cannot think of anything I wanted you to do on my behalf, and so none of it is my concern.'

And that is true, thought Mrs Deirdre Fount, I have said it and I do not care. I am not interested in where she went today. Mrs Oddicott caught sight of her daughter's expression and thought, she has hurt me, I am not to be thanked or made anything of, it was all done for nothing.

'I am used to being disregarded,' she said.

So help me, thought Deirdre Fount, *that* is not true at all. But she said only, 'I have finished the onions.'

Mrs Oddicott swept them off the dish and into the frying pan, without a word.

'I will make James's drink,' said Mrs Deirdre Fount.

'You will have to wait. If we are late with supper and James with his drink, well, that is only to be expected when the routine is so tumbled about. I cannot have you stretching across my path, getting in the way of the oven and sink. If the cooking is left to me then the least I can ask for is peace and quiet in which to get on with it.'

Deirdre Fount walked out of the kitchen, shutting the door very quickly, so that the draught blew the light out from under the frying pan with a sharp sound.

But I do not feel very pleased with myself, she thought, looking out of the sitting-room window on to the box hedge and the bay window of the houses opposite. I have kept a secret and it is no secret at all. For she had been nowhere, or nowhere of any consequence. She had sat for some time in the dome shelter, beside the miniature golf course, after deciding not to meet James, and it had been damp and unpleasant. Then, because she could think of nothing else to do, had trailed slowly down the cliff paths on to the sea front. The tide was out, the fog receding. It had been very cold. After a time, she had walked away from the upper residential part of the town and into the lower bay, where she had looked at closed cafés and shuttered arcades and piles of deckchairs laid up for the winter under green tarpaulin.

It had seemed an excitement, an act of defiance, to go out alone when she had promised to stay in, and to go without knowing where, without leaving any message behind her. But it was all a disappointment, new worlds had not opened to her, there had been no stranger, innocently met. In the end she had walked back through the town into the shopping parade and sat in a café for fifty minutes, being served with two cups of tea by an Irish waitress. Nobody else had come. The shops were closed. The walls of the café were papered with green and grey washable Moorish castles.

'Tea *only*?'

So she had had bread and butter and an iced cake, and made them last. If it had been summer, things would have been better, she could have defied Mrs Winifred Oddicott and mixed with the visitors, could have listened to conversations even if she had not managed to find her own, could have tried the penny amusements and weighed herself and eaten candy floss and looked at the blue sea.

But it was not summer. She paid her bill and walked slowly home, feeling restless and depressed, and fearing all the questions of her mother.

'Am I to put this food in the oven for you to keep warm, Deirdre, are you standing by the window for some time to come? Pay no attention to me, *I* do not mind eating alone, I am sure.'

Deirdre Fount followed her mother into the dining room. It is my own fault, she thought, I have brought it all upon myself.

Mrs Oddicott had removed the floral apron to eat her meal, but not the hat.

'Oh, this is all too ridiculous,' said Deirdre Fount, cutting a slice of wholemeal bread, 'we are grown women, let us behave as such. There is no room or time for petty quarrels.'

Mrs Winifred Oddicott stuffed her mouth very full of liver and potato, so that she might have time to keep her daughter waiting, while she considered the matter.

Upstairs in his room, James Fount wrote about magnetic properties and thought about his unknown father.

I am a man used to doing without sleep, Major Bertram Carpenter would say. I spend a large part of every night awake, I lie and think and am patient, nobody has ever heard me complain.

But he was sound asleep when the bedside telephone rang through the suite, sound asleep when his wife answered it, and she had a hard time of waking him. It was half-past three.

'Bertram, are you awake, dear? Do you follow what I am saying to you? It is Mr Isepp, dear.'

'Isepp, on the telephone in the middle of the night? Whatever are the hospital authorities thinking of, allowing this?'

'No, no, it is one of the nurses, I think, a sister in the hospital. Mr Isepp is very ill.'

'What? Of course Isepp is ill, I know perfectly well that he is ill. There can be no liaison between day and night staff, if someone has telephoned in the middle of the night simply to tell me that, when I have already visited him during the day.'

'No, no. They mean that he has taken a turn for the worse. His condition is giving rise to some anxiety, those were the words, I think. They feel you should be there – if you wish to go, that is. Someone should be there.'

Major Carpenter struggled with the bedclothes in order to sit up. The bottle-green pyjamas hung loosely over his elderly body.

'Now, Flora, what exactly did they say, can you recall their *precise* words? You are very bad with messages over the telephone and it is important, I am not being called out on some wild goose chase.'

Mrs Flora Carpenter patiently repeated the conversation she had had with the hospital sister, word for word.

'It seems to me that they are panicking, nevertheless,' said her husband, 'they are making a fuss over very little. It will not be necessary – I do not think I shall go.'

'Oh dear! Bertram, do you not think . . .'

'What?'

'Well, only that they *did* say "seriously ill".'

'I ask you to remember that *you* did not see Isepp today, and so you can have no true idea of his condition. I saw him and can form my own judgement. He looked poorly, certainly, but I was assured that he would pull round.'

'Very well, dear.'

'Perhaps it is Isepp himself, having no clear idea of night and day just at present, who has asked to see me, and they have taken this for a bad sign, they are pandering to the whims of a delirious man.'

Mrs Flora Carpenter shook her head, not willing to commit

herself to saying go, or, do not go, afraid that the consequences of either course would rebound upon her, and that she would be held to blame.

'No,' said Bertram Carpenter, 'I shall try and go back to sleep. Not that I am very likely to succeed, for I sleep very little. This is surely a false alarm.'

And he lay down again, pulling the bedclothes up around his stubbled chin.

Mrs Carpenter hesitated.

'Well,' he said, 'put out the light, let us have some rest if we can, what is the matter with you, Flora?'

Mrs Flora Carpenter put out the light, went back to her own bed and slept.

Major Carpenter did not sleep. He lay and thought of Isepp, alone in the bed of a public institution. Isepp is not a man to withstand that easily, he thought, he gives in, he is affected by all sorts of circumstances which any stronger man would ignore. It is a bad business altogether. Not that I can believe he is seriously ill, the doctor did not seem concerned and I am confident of having got the truth out of them all. No, but it is a question of company, of support, of his feeling that a friend is at hand, for he has always been able to talk freely to me, I can make him face up to things fairly and squarely, I can pull him through. Isepp needs a steadying influence.

And after three quarters of an hour, Major Bertram Carpenter had talked himself into getting up and going out to the hospital.

He was appalled to find that they had also taken it upon themselves to call the housekeeper, Mrs Momus. She sat beside Isepp's bed looking pinched and resentful.

'*She* is not a relative, she is not next-of-kin,' said Major Carpenter loudly to the nurse in the corridor. 'She is no more than a paid help, a daily woman, I cannot at all see why you should have found it necessary to bring her. Isepp will not be very pleased.'

'You will please keep your voice down, this is a hospital and it is five o'clock in the morning.'

Major Bertram Carpenter walked past her into Isepp's room, ignoring the housekeeper.

'Now, Isepp,' he said in a firm voice, determined to show that things had gone on long enough, and that, if he had been called out in the night, then they had better get to the bottom of things, discover the reason why.

'Now . . .'

The housekeeper got to her feet, appalled at the way he had blundered in and started to shout, and a nurse came into the room also, ready to protest.

Major Carpenter stopped and looked down at his friend in the narrow bed. Isepp's face was grey, there was a hoarse sound in his throat. Under the gaze of three people around his bed, he breathed a sudden, loud, strained breath and did not breathe again.

From outside in the corridor came the sound of a trolley, the swish of a closing door.

'Ah,' said Mrs Momus and lifted the handkerchief to her open mouth. 'Ah,' and she began to moan and rock herself to and fro, so that the nurse had to escort her from the room, leaving Major Carpenter alone with Isepp. Isepp's mouth was slightly open, his eyes closed.

He is dead, thought Major Carpenter, the man is dead. Now here is something . . . And his legs gave way under him, he sat down abruptly on the bedside chair. As a young man he had witnessed many deaths and never been afraid, it had been a thing apart from him, of which he was very scornful. The years had helped him to forget. Until now, and he was old, he was seventy-three and confronted with the body of his great friend, Isepp. Major Carpenter stared down at his own hands and noticed with surprise that they were no longer the hands of a young man. He was touched with a new realization of the truth of the matter, and a sudden fear.

'You will have to leave now, you must come out into the corridor. Come along, Major.'

'Do not touch me, Madam, I am not in need of your support, do not try to lead me along as if I were old and blind.'

In the corridor, the housekeeper wailed and snuffled into her handkerchief.

'That is not at all necessary,' said Major Carpenter, 'he was no relative of yours, he was only your employer. That is not part of your duty.'

'He was a good friend to me, a good friend,' said Mrs Momus and gave way to fresh tears.

Major Carpenter was appalled, but, seeing the doctor who had lied to him only the day before, he turned his attention away from Mrs Momus, and jumped forward; putting his back against Isepp's door, to bar the way.

'This is a fine thing,' he said, 'what happened? What lies did you have me believe? Why was I allowed to go carefree away from here, without a shadow of a doubt about my friend's condition, when you *knew* and kept that knowledge to yourself? Nothing was ever disclosed, you behave as though you were a secret society. But it is your duty to tell the truth to relatives and friends, those closest to your patients, for you do not own them, sir, they have only been entrusted to your professional care, for a limited time. You should admit us to your confidence, so that we may brace ourselves and be fully prepared.'

'Come, come now! Mr Isepp was an old man, he was very ill and frail. But I realize that you are in a state of shock. Let me go through.'

'You will stay and listen to me, sir. Because, so blithe was your attitude – and, let me say, that of his own practitioner – so glib was the talk of mild illness and getting better with antibiotics, that I am tempted to ask myself whether there has been some negligence. The man was not so very ill, you said so yourself, and yet he came here and you attended to him and he died.'

'Sister Meredith, would you . . .'

'Do not evade me, sir, do not refuse to look me in the eye. My friend Isepp is dead, there is nothing you can do to help him now, do you hear me? He is dead and he should still be alive.'

'You are very shocked. I will call an ambulance and have you taken home.'

'You will do nothing, you will not lay a hand upon me. I will walk from this building while I have my health and strength, I will not suffer as my friend Isepp has suffered at your hands, I will not travel in one of your ambulances, for all the world to see.'

In the chair, the housekeeper sat and stared out of damp eyes, and continued to rock herself, to and fro.

Major Bertram Carpenter walked, stamping his feet hard, down the drive and out into the avenue, trying to beat the dust of the hospital off his shoes. It was ten minutes to six on a November morning, dark and bitterly cold. He walked and walked, and it was two miles to the Prince of Wales Hotel. His hands shook and his mouth worked, and the dead, grey face of Isepp was before him, and in his ears, the short, ragged breath that he had so suddenly taken.

Soon have him on his feet – what feet he has, eh? Patch him up and send him home, nothing to worry about, no need to be at all anxious. No, I daresay that you are right. That was what they had said, the smooth-tongued, bland-faced professional men.

Something might have been done, said Major Carpenter, as he rounded the dark bend of the road and came out on to the Esplanade, where a raw spray blew into his face from off the sea. He walked unsteadily, unsure of his own balance. Something should have been done. Isepp ought not to be dead.

Chapter Five

MRS FLORA CARPENTER sat beside her husband on the green chintz sofa. Her hands lay in her lap and she pulled the rings fretfully up and down her fingers. Major Carpenter stared out of the window into space.

'*Something*, dear,' Mrs Carpenter was saying, 'if only a cup of tea. You must take something.'

Major Carpenter did not reply.

'You had no breakfast and no lunch, you say that you cannot eat. But a drink, one cup of tea surely . . .'

He made an impatient gesture with his head.

'For me. Try and take something just to set my mind at rest, Bertram. It is so painful to watch, and I cannot think that Mr Isepp would approve, he would not want you to starve and mourn in quite this extreme way. You are doing him no service.'

'Isepp is dead,' said Major Bertram Carpenter, in a dull voice.

'Yes, dear, and I am so very sorry. I have said so.'

Although, she thought, he was old and ill and lonely, and there is nothing wrong with the quiet, quick death of someone so very old. He lived out his life, it is all in accordance with nature. That is how we may die some day. *Some* day . . .

She had been shocked at the way her husband had taken it, at the expression on his face when he had arrived home at dawn and the way he had sat here all day, gazing out to sea or into space, only shaking his head from time to time. His flesh had gone a curious putty colour. She did not think that even when their own daughter had died, at the age of fifteen months, he had been so preoccupied with grief. Neither had she realized that he had felt so close to the man Isepp.

'Do not sit over me, Flora,' he said suddenly, flapping a hand, 'do not hang about.'

'Where shall I go?'

'Go? Go anywhere, go out, go away. Go into the other room or down into the lounge to have tea with the wives of Jewish tradesmen.'

'Tea has already been brought up here, Bertram.'

'Go *anywhere*. I do not mind, but I will not have you sitting over me.'

'I am worried, dear, you are so unlike yourself. You came in at such a time this morning, I am wondering whether you have caught a chill and are now running a temperature. You will not eat or walk out, I have never seen you behave in this way.'

'You are seeing me now,' he said heavily, 'you are seeing me now. I have not the heart for anything.' And then, Major Carpenter hit his fist down into the palm of the other hand, and his weak blue eyes were filled with anger and fear.

'It should not have happened,' he shouted at his wife, 'not enough care was taken of him. Something could have been done.'

'But . . .'

'Isepp or anyone else, it is all the same. We are helpless in the hands of those men, *they* decide, they are the ones who have power over life and death, and we can do nothing. Isepp is dead, I watched him die and I was helpless. It is all too late.'

Mrs Flora Carpenter got up and walked away from him, moving a book from one table to another, adjusting a cushion, for he frightened her, when he shouted, she would rather have him silent, after all.

There was also the question, which she had not dared to raise, of the dinner invitations. The previous evening, they had been written and posted, and tomorrow morning, they would fall through letter-boxes on to mats in various homes of Westbourne. But perhaps Major Carpenter would not now want to go on with the arrangements. She looked over at him and tried to order her thoughts, to decide what was best to do. The dinner party was for the following week and there was no possible reason for it to be cancelled. It was not as though Mr Isepp had been a relative. But Major Carpenter sat so still and stared out of the window into space and was plainly not himself, not to be appealed to without a good deal of thought.

'Perhaps I will just go downstairs, Bertram,' said Mrs Carpenter uncertainly, 'if you really will not take any tea?'

He lifted his head and looked at her for a moment with a blank expression. Death, thought Major Carpenter, death has come to Isepp, he will know everything there is to know about it. All must die.

'Yes,' Mrs Carpenter said when he did not make any reply. 'Well . . .' and she quickly left the room.

On the second floor, in the corridor outside the Blue Lounge, Mrs Carpenter almost bumped into the salesman. He had a ginger moustache. Mrs Carpenter inclined her head to him very slightly, for she did not want to be openly rude to any guests, no matter what her husband might say.

'Good afternoon,' said the man, whose name was Aubrey Fount, and held open the swing doors to let her pass.

Mrs Winifred Oddicott picked the letter off the mat and turned it over. She could see that it only contained a slim sheet of paper. She held it in her hand and the writing on the envelope was quite unfamiliar, but the pads of her fingers felt over the crest embossed on the back of it.

'Come, James, finish your kipper and then go upstairs to clean your teeth. You will be late.'

There were almost seven minutes before James Fount was due to leave the house.

'It is only twenty past,' he said, nipping off little pieces of the crust of toast, nip, nip, nip with his front teeth.

'Do not eat like a rabbit, James. And the kitchen clock is slow.'

'*How* slow?'

'Some minutes, I think. Enough for you to be late, and that is never a good thing.'

'I shall switch on the radio and find out *really* what time it is.'

'You will leave the radio alone, you will go upstairs now and clean your teeth. I will not be contradicted.'

'You were not being.'

'Or have my word doubted by my own grandson who is only eleven years old.'

For she wanted him to be out of the way so that she could be alone with her daughter when the letter was opened.

'Pick your feet up, James. Now, your dinner money is in the front pocket of your satchel, be careful with it.'

James Fount looked at her with scorn from beneath his thick lashes. 'I have another four minutes at *least,*' he said.

Mrs Oddicott heard him trailing very slowly up the stairs just as his mother came down.

'Oh,' said Deirdre Fount, 'is it kippers? I am not sure that I feel like eating kippers this morning.'

'Then if I may say so, you should have told me sooner. You could smell them cooking, I am sure, you might even have seen them in the refrigerator yesterday. But you do not speak out, you cannot be bothered, you wait until I have them carefully cooked and buttered.'

'Surely you can eat two?'

'That would be very greedy.'

'Well then, *be* greedy. Is there any post for us this morning?'

'I suffer enough with indigestion after every meal, *you* have never experienced that, or you would not tell me so glibly to eat two kippers. Kippers of all things!'

'Why, of all things?' Deirdre Fount poured milk from the bottle into the jug. 'I thought I heard the click of the letter-box while I was in the bathroom.'

'Kippers are smoked and all smoked things are *highly* indigestible.'

'Then you should never eat them at all, should you? I shall boil myself an egg.'

'There is not room for two of us at the stove, how often do I have to tell you that? I suppose I must boil you an egg.'

'Very well,' said Deirdre Fount, for it was too early to begin an argument of any kind, and she did not find it worthwhile to have ill feeling before the day had so much as begun. 'I will have a kipper after all.'

'Oh, not just on *my* account I hope. Do not eat what you have no taste for simply to please me.'

'No, it is to please myself. Is *that* a letter, there beside the teapot?'

Mrs Winifred Oddicott blocked the way with her pan of steaming kippers.

'You were wrong,' said James Fount, appearing suddenly in the doorway.

'I *did* have five minutes and there is nothing slow about this kitchen clock.'

Mrs Oddicott laid down her fish slice. There was a little silence.

'Well,' she said at last, 'if your own mother does not correct you, I am afraid that I shall. That is no way to talk to me, to contradict and speak so uppishly. Anyone can make a mistake. I was only thinking of you and not wanting you to be in trouble at school.'

James stared, not at her but away over her left shoulder, at a little spot on the wall below the calendar of Our Lakeland Heritage.

'Nobody says anything if you are late,' he said, 'nothing happens. You just miss prayers, that's all.'

'*That* does not seem to me at all a proper way of going on, if you are telling me the truth. They are supposed to be training you in a sense of personal responsibility, to be fitting you for adult life. That is why we pay such high fees at Westbourne Priors School, for the extra lessons, over and above what is merely scholastic. Punctuality is one of the first signs of a good character.'

James Fount turned away. 'I wasn't *going* to be late,' he said, 'anyway.'

He picked up his lunch apple and left the kitchen.

'I notice that he does not even kiss his mother, these days, let alone me, he does not so much as say goodbye.'

'He is too big to be kissed, he would be embarrassed.'

'What nonsense!' Mrs Winifred Oddicott took up her knife and fork, and then laid them down again.

'Why, there is a letter for you, Deirdre! It has been standing beside the teapot for some time. Are you not going to open it? Are you not interested in a letter sent from someone at the Prince of Wales Hotel?'

'Oh, now here is a parcel from the wool firm,' said Mrs Deirdre Fount, and she bent over it eagerly with the scissors. Away in a dark corner of the shop, Mrs Oddicott sorted crochet patterns noisily.

'Perhaps it is that green wool for Miss Collins – and not before time, she has been waiting quite three weeks. It is too bad, I have already sent out two postcards to remind them. When it is only a small quantity they simply cannot be bothered. The delivery time stretches out and stretches out and sometimes I wonder what they *do* with our orders in between receiving and attending to them. Oh – there now, it is *not* the green wool, it is something quite different after all. Samples, by the looks of things, as if the traveller does not bring quite enough, tempting us to buy. Yes, specimen hanks of "a new light-weight lustre wool, in black and gold, or white and silver, ideal for delicate evening tops, lace-stitch stoles and, etc." Yes well, that is *very* nice. Don't you think it is nice, mother? Very nice. It has a lovely sparkle and such a soft feel.'

Mrs Winifred Oddicott did not turn round.

'Mother? Come over to the light and just glance at it. I wonder if we should order some, if it would come in time for Christmas? Though really, it is already rather late and they are so dilatory, I would not like to risk being left with large quantities through the summer. What do you think?'

Mrs Oddicott's fingers went flick flick flick, over the edges of the crochet patterns.

'Oh, dear, how silly this all is,' exclaimed Deirdre Fount, turning the wool anxiously over in her hand. 'Why will you not answer? As if it were all somehow my fault that you are feeling snubbed. I am sure there is no need to bear a grudge.'

'I begrudge you nothing, Deirdre, I never have.'

'Yes, you begrudge my invitation to dinner with the Carpenters, that is why there is this frostiness towards me this morning.'

'The *Carpenters*! Oh dear me, you say it as if they were Royalty! And who are the Carpenters? A pair of old fogies, rich enough to live in a luxury hotel and only able to win friends for themselves by providing expensive dinners. Not that the food in any hotel, whether the Prince of Wales or where you please, is likely to be anything marvellous, for I daresay everything is frozen and pre-cooked. I notice that Major and Mrs Carpenter have always to buy their companions these days, I have not seen that son visiting them for quite some time.'

'I think it is kind of them to invite me, they are very generous people and most thoughtful. It is all the more welcome for being so unexpected.'

Mrs Winifred Oddicott had now come forward and was facing her daughter across the counter.

'Unexpected? Now do not tell me that you have not hoped for this, for I will beg to contradict you, Deirdre, you are my own daughter and no one knows you better than I. You have been trying to curry favour with the Carpenters all this summer past, you have angled for an invitation and I only hope that now it has come you will make the most of it. You had better buy yourself a new outfit to go off to the Prince of Wales Hotel.'

She picked up the packet of wool samples. 'It is shoddy,' she said at once, 'cheap and vulgar looking. I am surprised you should not see that at once. Anything that glitters or has some kind of *sheen* is not really quite ... well, it would be almost like wearing sequins. I will not have any of it in my shop.'

Deirdre Fount, humiliated and angry that the edge had been so successfully taken off her pleasure in the forthcoming dinner party, leaned over the counter towards her mother. 'You are jealous,' she said, and her face grew flushed, 'you are jealous of your own daughter! What a different story it would have been if *you* were invited – we should never hear the last. But you are not invited, you are not wanted there, and so you do your best to spoil my pleasure. And the life I am obliged to live in this town is not exactly a cornucopia of pleasures. But I will not be beaten down by your petty remarks, I will go and I will enjoy myself, I will think nothing of you.' She heard the last little shriek of her own voice and then there was a terrible silence in the drapery shop. Mrs Winifred Oddicott stood very still, her face set and her mouth working a little at the corners.

At last, she said in a peculiar voice, 'I am very glad to know your mind, Deirdre, I am glad you have let your true feelings about me come to the surface. And if you do not mind, I think I would rather not stay longer in the shop with you, I think I will go quietly home. When I have done so, you will perhaps come to realize what you have said and how it has affected me.'

A hank of the black and gold lustre wool rolled suddenly off the end of the counter on to the shop floor.

Deirdre Fount burst into tears.

Aubrey Fount had never imagined that he might *want* to take his annual holiday in November, but when it came to it, he was glad of the opportunity, and most relieved that he had not, after all, gone to Majorca in the summer. It gave him an excuse, although he did not in fact say, 'I am taking my holiday,' in so many words.

The woman called Miriam, to whom he had only gone for sympathy and the comforts of the flesh, had let him down badly and quite without warning. After fifteen easy months she had become demanding. Aubrey Fount had not thought she was that type at all, he had chosen so carefully, and she had seemed to know exactly what kind of relationship he had in mind for them. Miriam was a widow and full of understanding, who managed a dress shop in Birmingham and wore black jersey suits with blouses cut low over a full bosom. Miriam had a house of her own and a small car and a teenage daughter, and said that she valued her independence. Until now.

'I am forty-three,' she had said to him one evening, 'I have to think of the future.'

And, 'It is all very well for you, but a woman needs more, after a time, a woman needs security when she loves a man.'

And, 'If this is to be all, perhaps I would be better off looking somewhere else, Aubrey, for I am not the young girl I was, the days race by.'

And, 'It is so *unsatisfying*, dear. I have so much to offer you.'

Aubrey Fount had begun to panic.

'You know how I am placed,' he had said, in a voice that begged for sensitive understanding, 'if only it were different, if only I were able to decide for myself alone, if I were a free man.'

'You are divorced, she has no claim upon you.'

'No, no, but I still feel responsible, Miriam, I feel that I am needed, because of the boy.' For he had elaborated upon Deirdre's position of helplessness and had not disclosed that for eight years he had had nothing to do with them.

'It is all very difficult.'

At this point, he had taken Miriam's hand fondly. They were

sitting in a red-plush and mirrored scampi bar on a Saturday night. Miriam wore dusky pink grosgrain with a silver-fox collar and bits of diamanté in her piled-up hair. Aubrey Fount held her hand for some time and looked at her with feeling. He had a small, pink mouth beneath the ginger moustache.

'I have too many ties,' he said, 'I have explained it to you so often. That is why I value you so much, because *you* are not a tie, I feel at ease with you, you make me free as no one else can.'

Miriam looked doubtful. I have heard this before, she would say to him when he had finished, it is an old story and no longer good enough for me.

'Miriam, we are friends, good friends.'

Miriam did not reply.

'You have given me such a lot, you have helped me when I have badly needed help. But I beg you for your own sake not to get too involved with me, not to become dependent, I am the wrong man.'

'Well ...'

'Please. Just for the time being, Miriam. Until things are clearer, until I can feel free. It is not too much to ask, surely.'

'Oh – very well, no, I suppose it is not.'

And for the rest of the evening, she had put her hand reassuringly over his and been her warm and welcoming self, had seemed to accept everything, after all. But later on, it began again, the hinting and a few tears now and again, the odd, bitter remark. Aubrey Fount had woken in the night thinking about it.

It will be better to get away for a time, he decided, show that I mean what I say, I cannot have her emotional dependence. He had arranged to take his holiday, he had borrowed the company's newest six-seater American saloon – perhaps, he said, he might combine business with pleasure and if he could serve the firm in any way ... He had written a note to Miriam.

'My son,' he wrote, '... illness ... need to see me ... make some arrangements ... business matters ... you will understand and think of me ... I have no choice ...'

Well, thought Aubrey Fount, it is not entirely untrue, for at the back of my mind for some time has been the idea of visiting James, I have felt guilty and now I am listening to the voice of conscience. I have evaded my responsibilities in that direction for too long.

He was uncertain whether or not he wanted to see Deirdre again. He was curious, that was all. She was almost forty now, and he thought that middle age would not be kind to her. He wanted to reassure himself that he had missed nothing. Since the divorce, he had been travelling about a good deal and perhaps it had been best not to disturb the situation, although he had been granted free access to the boy. But Mrs Winifred Oddicott had written him a sharp letter about his not interfering, because a child needed stability, security in the home, odd visits could do nothing but harm. Aubrey Fount had been relieved. The boy had been taken over completely by the two women from the moment of his birth, he seemed to have nothing at all to do with his father.

But now, he thought, James is eleven years old, a growing boy who might welcome my interest and affection. And he turned the six-seater American saloon in the direction of Westbourne. On the journey, he became a little maudlin about the boy. We are father and son, he said, overtaking an articulated lorry, we will shake hands firmly and have a great deal to say to one another, there will be questions he will want to ask me, there is the truth to be told to him as only a man can tell it. I will give him advice and console him if he feels dominated by those women.

But he had no clear idea of how he might approach James. He would have to find Deirdre and obtain her permission, and he had only one address now, that of the drapery shop which they had taken over soon after moving into the town. From that day, no communication had passed between Mrs Oddicott and her daughter and Aubrey Fount, although every Christmas and birthday he sent the boy a pound note in an envelope addressed only to him.

They may even have moved on to another town, the journey may be entirely wasted, thought Aubrey Fount, and winked at the girl working a petrol pump. He wondered if there were some legal ban on a divorced woman moving the child without giving his father a new address, whether or not she had custody.

Well, at least he would spend his money on comfort at the

best – the Prince of Wales – hotel. He would be entirely alone, he decided, for Miriam had frightened him, he had no desire to be with a woman. The petrol pump girl brought his change and let him squeeze her hand.

He would meet his son and take him out to a stylish lunch and teach him about the wine and hear of his triumphs at school, his plans for the future. He would read and go for bracing walks, he would spend an entirely honourable holiday.

All of which he remembered as he sat in the Laurel Leaf Café, opposite the draper's shop, waiting for Mrs Oddicott to come out for a short time. He had preferred not to telephone or send a card, he wanted to walk in upon Deirdre and enjoy her surprise. But he had already sat here on two mornings and Mrs Oddicott had stayed inside the shop. Perhaps he would have to face her, after all. Aubrey Fount ordered another cup of coffee and decided to telephone, after all, and perhaps arrange to meet the boy from school one afternoon, see nobody but him.

The door of the shop opened and Mrs Winifred Oddicott emerged. She looked pale, and the sight of her, the way she was walking, the set of her jaw and the navy-blue felt hat brought depressing memories back to Aubrey Fount. She had not changed, not in the slightest, she was the same awful old woman.

He stood up quickly and paid his bill.

'Speak up, speak clearly, Flora, I cannot understand what you are trying to say, you mutter and mumble so, and let us have the light on if you please, I never hear properly in the dark.'

Mrs Carpenter had summoned up her courage to speak to him at the end of the television news, when they sat side by side watching a blank screen. It is a decadent habit to watch television after ten-thirty at night, Major Carpenter said, we are left with no time for quietness and conversation before bed. And so she had asked him about the dinner party.

'Because, Bertram, I do not see however we would explain it if we had to cancel the invitations – so rude. It is not as though it coincides with the funeral or anything of that kind, and everyone will wonder, because, as I have pointed out, Mr Isepp was not a relative. The dinner party is a whole week away, after all. But I thought that I would mention it to you, dear, I only wanted to know how you feel. You have been so – well, you have not been quite yourself this past week.'

All this she said as she stood with her hand on the light switch, and looked uncertainly down at her husband. She was a small, pastel woman, there was always the faint bloom as of pale powder settled on her, not only upon her skin but over her whole person, her clothes and shoes and the whitish grey stockings. Mrs Flora Carpenter was beautiful as an old woman, as she had been a beautiful girl, she wore her hair curled flat against her brow like a Thomas Hardy heroine.

Major Bertram Carpenter turned a little in his chair and stared hard.

'Flora, what are you talking about? I have not understood one word you have been saying, I do not follow your thoughts.'

'The *dinner* party, dear.'

'Someone has invited us to a dinner party? How very tactless. Please write them a simple, polite note of refusal, for *we* cannot go to any dinner parties. Or I cannot, that is to say, and I would hope that you feel the same way. I have no heart for anything. This is not a time for entertainment, for over-eating and the drinking of alcohol, my friend Isepp is dead. I do not want to go out to anybody's dinner parties.'

Mrs Flora Carpenter sat down beside him, took his hand into hers and patted it. He has aged, she thought sadly, in these few days he has aged suddenly. I look at him and see that he is an old man.

'*Our* dinner party, Bertram, I am speaking about our party here, next Thursday evening. Perhaps it has slipped your mind, you have had so much to think about and been so very upset. But I have already sent out the invitations, they were written and posted the day before Mr Isepp died. That is what I have been trying to tell you, and to ask if everything shall go forward as arranged, if you see any real need to cancel it altogether, in spite of your own personal sadness. Though I suppose it might be deferred, that would not be quite so impolite. Yes, I had not thought of that.'

'*We* are not giving any dinner parties. What "arrangements"? This is the first I have heard of any of it. So you have made plans without so much as consulting me, you are going your own way, after all these years. This is a fine thing, Flora, a fine thing!'

Tears of frustration and bewilderment came into the eyes of Mrs Flora Carpenter, although her husband stared at the floor and tapped his feet angrily, thinking of the death of Isepp, and did not notice them. I am to die, he thought, I am to die alone. There were men and women and children dying, in battle and flood and famine on the television news, and I too will die. All must die.

'If only you could just give your whole mind to it, Bertram, try and remember that we discussed it in detail together.'

'I am quite sure that we did not.'

'It was you who suggested that we should invite Mrs Fount.'

'*I* know what I remember, Flora,' said Major Carpenter, lifting his head and looking her straight in the eyes, 'I am not entirely senile, my wits have not quite gone, you see, I cannot easily be deceived. I remember what I said on the ship as we were sailing towards Barbados. I said that there were to be no more dinner parties, that I have grown tired of the people of Westbourne taking it for granted that they would feed at my table all the year round. I said that we would retire and eat alone. I have no longer any time for chattering companions. *That* is what I said, I am quite clear about it in my mind. And now it is time that we were in bed. Where are the hot drinks? Have you rung down for them?'

Well then, thought Mrs Carpenter sadly, I must write letters to everyone, I must explain as best I can and apologize, there will be no more dinner parties. But she wondered where it was all to end, this grief of her husband's, his restlessness and strange behaviour. He sat about their suite all day long and would not read, not even the letters and obituaries in the *Daily Telegraph*, nor play chess nor talk to her, he would not go down into the public rooms. Except when he grew suddenly tired of her company and she could escape to the pillar box or to tea, she was confined within their suite, all their meals were brought up to them. Twice only Major Carpenter had ventured outside. He had walked a short way along the sea front and back again, hands behind him and eyes on the ground. Sometimes he would burst out wildly about Isepp and his death and the negligence of doctors. The funeral was tomorrow.

Mrs Flora Carpenter got carefully to her feet, which were stiff with pain from rheumatism, these damp, cold days. So there will be no dinner party, she thought, there will perhaps be nothing more to look forward to, we shall have no social life, our horizons will shrink and shrink.

The hot drinks came.

At half-past five, Deirdre Fount locked up the shop, knowing that she dared not yet go home. It had been a bad day, too many things had happened, she was confused, afraid and distressed.

She went back inside, in her grey tweed coat and the autumn leaf headscarf, and sat down weakly on the customer's stool in the darkness. Across the street, the lights from the Laurel Leaf Café shone out blurred with steam.

'It was pretty awful coffee,' he had said, 'and pretty awful tea the other afternoon as well. But I was not coming in here so long as your mother held the fort.'

'No. No, of course.'

Deirdre Fount had held on to the round measuring stick and slipped it up and down between her fingers and her eyes had suddenly glazed over, she was unable to focus properly, after the shock of seeing him.

'What a place,' he had said, 'this Westbourne. Dead and alive hole, nothing to do, I can't think how you stand it, Deirdre. Full of old people dying off. Everyone's thrown in the sponge, it seems to me.'

And you, he had thought, you will soon be one of them, you are half-way down that slippery slope now, you and your mother. You have given in, there is no life in you. He thought of Miriam – two or three years older than Deirdre. Perhaps it had something to do with flesh. Miriam had flesh and to spare. Deirdre seemed to have none, no soft layer between skin and bone. He looked at her and thought of Miriam again with relief. And how long her skirts are, he thought, half-way down her calves. If she has no one to tell her about her dowdiness, has she not the wit to see it for herself, has she no feminine pride? She stood on the other side of the counter in a tucked blouse, and her skin was the beige colour of women who never make up, never comfort themselves with cream and lotion and sun and love.

But there must once have been something more than this, some spark of youth or sexual promise to have led him on. He could not remember, he had no picture in his mind of Deirdre Oddicott who had married him at the age of twenty-five.

In those days, Deirdre herself thought now, as she sat among the silks and safety-pins in the darkness, I was hopeful and excited about life, in those days I wanted to try and please a man, I wore padded brassières and shaved my legs and matched up the bright colours of fabrics against my skin and hair, in those days I was very conscious of all my shortcomings and I made an effort. In those days . . . but she could not remember what had happened in between or when the change had begun.

'Well, long time no see,' he had said, walking rather spryly into the empty shop, ding-dinging at the bell. She had been in the back room, wiping her face after the crying. 'And how has life been treating you, Deirdre?'

A man of the world, she had thought as a girl, a man who knows his way about, a man who is climbing the first rungs on the ladder of success, an outgoing, popular, sociable man. But because she had prided herself on her sensitivity she had fancied that she saw the frailty there, too, behind the masculine assurance, the ordinary human need. She had wanted to be his comfort and refuge, the quiet background to his success. I will look after you, she had thought, but I will let it seem to be you who is looking after me. I will not let you down.

He had paced about the small shop. 'Plenty you could do here to brighten up a bit, Deirdre,' he said, 'open out that front and organize your display. Windows, that is what you need, take my advice, I know about these things. Plenty of windows.'

He had always been so full of ideas and not only for himself. She had listened and tried to understand and encourage and now, as he poked about among the stock and criticized, she was both affronted because he could know so little about any of it, and excited for he was right, he did not mince matters, was not afraid to point out the need for change. They could do so much more here, she had always thought so, expand the business in a number of directions. She had long had a vision of what they might achieve.

'My mother . . .' she had said to him.

'All right, don't tell me!'

'Oh, but I do welcome your opinions, it is all very helpful. Tell me whatever you think should be done.'

He had not bothered, after that.

In the end, she had managed to say, 'Why have you come here? Why do you want to see me? I suppose that you are just passing through, selling your cars.'

'No. I have taken my annual holiday. That is why I am here.'

And then he had sat down and unbuttoned his overcoat and spoken earnestly across the counter to her about the boy.

'It has been on my conscience, I admit it to you, Deirdre, it has worried me. I see a duty, a duty I have neglected. Oh yes, I do not deny that, there is no need to put a good face on things. But in the end, I knew that I had to do it, I had to come here. I am his father, there is no getting away from that, I have behaved very badly.'

Deirdre Fount flushed and stared down at the drawers full of foundation garments directly beneath the glass counter.

'It is high time I saw the boy, talked to him – he is growing up, he needs a man's influence. I have not been all that I should be, I admit it freely. If there is any guilt, then lay it at my door.'

He speaks as he always used to speak, thought Deirdre Fount, he looks at me frankly and makes plain, honest remarks and I believe him as I always used to believe him. I see sincerity in his eyes though my mother tried hard to sow the seeds of doubt very early on in our married life. A smooth tongue, Mrs Winifred Oddicott had said, he talks himself into things and out of things, it is all sleight of hand. I am surprised you cannot see it, Deirdre, for I have never trusted him. But you were always gullible, even as a small child you were too easy with your trust and sympathy, I had to warn you time after time. It is a very good thing I am here to save you from yourself. And she had been beside herself with anger when she had failed to save her from the unsuitable marriage to Aubrey Fount.

I am being persuaded again, she thought, but not against my

better judgement for he is plainly quite sincere in what he says. He had no need to come here, he was not expected, it has been a very long time. He could have taken a holiday anywhere else, abroad perhaps, in the sun. But he recognizes that he has duties and responsibilities towards James and he is prepared to make up for the past. And he may well be right, James may need him very much now that he is eleven years old and that I do not altogether understand him.

'Of course I couldn't have taken the boy without asking your permission, coming to see you. Bygones are bygones, I hope, I bear nobody any malice, Deirdre, life is too short. Besides, I was interested in what kind of a life *you* have made for yourself.'

And you can see now, thought Deirdre Fount, you can see for yourself. I am a middle-aged woman living among other women, my mother rules the roost and I have nothing at all to hope for. You can see.

I am sorry for you, he thought, although you have only yourself to blame. I can see that you no longer bother to make an effort, you take no pride in yourself, you do not bother to disguise your lack of breasts, your dingy skin and grey hairs because you have given up hoping.

'A woman should always take care of herself,' Miriam had once said, 'she should *never* give in, it is a question of pride.'

'I can see that you are nice and comfortable,' Aubrey Fount had said aloud, 'a nice little shop, quite a pleasant town to live in, for all nothing appears to go on, and near the sea, good fresh air. Yes, I am glad it is no struggle for you to live. There are no hard feelings, you see, nothing of that kind. We are civilized, adult people.'

'Oh, there are many worse off,' she had said, turning round to push one of the drawers in the stand more firmly shut, 'I have a great deal to be thankful for, my life could be much worse.'

Aubrey Fount had begun to talk about the outing with James, and then customers had come in, he had buttoned his overcoat and left rather hurriedly. She would think about it, she had said, talk to James and then telephone to make arrangements.

Deirdre Fount looked out of the window at the other, darkened shops on the opposite side of the street, and tried to think about it now. It had been strangely easy while he had been standing in front of her, she had been quite calm after the initial shock and they had spoken together in rather bright, public voices. But now all her memories of present and past were jumbled together, they alarmed her and she did not know what she was going to decide or how she should approach James, a full realization of what had happened that afternoon came upon her. What shall I do, thought Mrs Deirdre Fount, and then she said it aloud in the silent shop. What shall I do?

She could not go home yet, either, could not walk into the house and speak to her mother as though everything were as usual, for Mrs Oddicott would see at once and she would have to confess, there would be astonishment and indignation and a swift decision.

She stood on the corner by the wine store and wondered where she might go. There was the Laurel Leaf Café. But he had been there earlier and she would not be able to think clearly because of it, she might accidentally sit upon the same chair that he had used, which would be a kind of indecency, almost a fleshly contact. There is nowhere, thought Deirdre Fount. But on the corner of the Esplanade she came upon the wedding-cake façade of the Majestic Hotel, which was quite suitable for a woman alone, and so she pulled her coat a little more tightly up around her neck, and went up the steps and inside.

Chapter Six

'WHAT have you been doing all this time?' asked Mrs Auriole Carpenter, whose face had a tight, polished look after removal of the overnight skin mask. 'The toast is quite hard now.'

Water from the tap she had just turned on drummed down into the stainless steel sink.

'There is something wrong with my razor,' said Edward Carpenter, who wore brown Harris tweed because it was his day for Country Properties.

'It is not six months old, nothing can possibly be wrong with it.'

'I do not say these things to amuse myself.'

'It was an expensive razor, I bought the one that cost most money so that it should *never* have anything wrong with it, and the toast should never have to be left to go hard.'

'A high price and efficiency do not always go hand in hand.'

'Am I to make fresh toast?'

'No, no. I see there is no letter from the boys. They reach the age of twelve and thirteen and forget about writing to their parents.'

'But parents do not forget about writing to their children, no matter what their age. There is a letter from your mother.'

'Ah!'

'And what can she have to write to us about in the middle of the week? I suppose we have done something that does not please them, she will have some remark to make about my shortcomings.'

Edward Carpenter clicked his tongue and took a long time over opening the envelope. My mother, he would have said, does not make remarks about you, my mother knows better than that, it is the prime concern of her old age to keep the peace and have a harmonious family. But there was much that he thought and did not say. He read the letter.

'It seems that something is not quite right with father.'

Mrs Auriole Carpenter stared out of the picture windows on to the landscape garden and the November rain, and thought about Lady Huntley's charity bazaar.

'I hope we are not expected to trail to Westbourne at this time of year, I hope there is not going to be another winter of illnesses and alarm. I have a great deal to do, I have been entrusted with all sorts of responsibilities and people do not care to be let down.'

'A friend of father's has died, it seems that he is taking it badly. It has been a great shock, she says.'

'I am sure I cannot think why. They are old people, they must expect their friends to start dying around them.'

'But perhaps when you are in your seventies . . .'

'Oh, I shall be quite sensible, quite clear-sighted, you need not worry about me on that score. There is no use trying to bury one's head in the sand at that or at any age,' said Mrs Auriole Carpenter who, for the past six years, had admitted to being thirty-five.

'Mother seems to be in need of some advice and a steadying hand. Perhaps I ought to go.'

'You have a job to do, you cannot afford the time to dash a hundred and fifty miles at the drop of a hat every time they feel low-spirited.'

'I think it is more than that, I doubt if they would ask if it were not rather serious.'

'This is awful toast, awful! I doubt if even the birds will manage to eat it.'

'Mother offers to book us into the hotel for a long weekend – as their guests, you know – we could keep an eye on them and it would be, she says, a little treat.'

'Well, it *is* a very pleasant hotel.' Mrs Carpenter refilled the Spode coffee pot. 'They allow themselves every luxury.'

'Apparently next weekend we could have the Gold Suite, which is not very often vacant.'

Mrs Auriole Carpenter sighed. 'If it is a case of family need then,' she said, 'if there is nothing else for it, then I suppose that Lady Huntley's committee will excuse me.'

Edward Carpenter smiled.

'I must say that we have always been very comfortable at the Prince of Wales Hotel.'

She buttered a second slice of the unsatisfactory toast.

In the end, she decided that it was not a pot of tea and tiny cakes on a silver tray that she needed, it was alcohol, a glass of medium dry sherry.

But people will stare at me, thought Deirdre Fount, they are quite sure to make remarks to one another, for it is unseemly of a woman to go into a hotel and drink alone, the worst is always assumed.

Yet there were, after all, hotels *and* hotels and this one was perfectly suitable, it had a high reputation for comfort and a large number of permanent residents, widows and spinsters. They must drink alone from time to time, she thought, they will think nothing of it. Though she hoped that she would not meet any acquaintances who could then say, there is poor Mrs Deirdre Fount, sitting alone over her sherry.

But the lounges were almost empty, it was the quiet hour between tea and dinner. Upstairs, innumerable baths were being taken, innumerable lace dresses were being laid out upon beds. Deirdre Fount sat down and unbuttoned her coat and took her diary and the gilt pencil out of her handbag, for it would be best if she could look preoccupied. Nobody would then suspect her of lingering in the hopes of attracting company.

What I need, she thought, making a ring neatly around the date of James's birthday, is a holiday. Not because I want a rest but for a change, a completely different atmosphere, new faces and stimulating conversation. And what I do *not* want is to be accompanied by my mother.

The sherry arrived and nobody came into the lounge, nobody paid her any attention.

I need to take a holiday with James, for I spend so little time with my son, he is growing away from me and he does not know my mind, I do not know his. If I am to salvage a little of our relationship for the future, I can only do it when my attention is not being distracted by my mother and my time is all his. Perhaps I have been a bad mother, perhaps *this* is bad, to sit in the brown lounge of the Majestic Hotel drinking sherry at six o'clock in the evening, when I might so easily be at home, listening to some story about an event at school or asking pertinent questions about his homework. He is both too much alone and too much with my mother. Like me, like me.

So we will go away.

Someone came into the lounge, hovered in the doorway. Deirdre Fount bent her head and quickly wrote, 'The Feast of St Michael and All Angels' in the space under September 29. The lounge doors swung shut again.

We will take a week's holiday and we will take it soon – in the time James has left after Christmas. Yet I cannot leave my mother alone with the shop, that would hardly be fair. Although she knew that she could, that the shop could easily have been managed by one person permanently, and that the two of them exhausted themselves tidying unnecessary cupboards, checking and re-checking the stock room.

The point was that Mrs Oddicott should not be left with any cards in her hand, she should not be given a chance to complain about all the extra work and worry and responsibility.

We will *close* the shop, said Deirdre Fount, we will both take a week's holiday; the customers will not mind for that is just what so many of them have often told us to do. 'You are looking tired, you are a little pale, take a holiday, Mrs Fount, and you will feel a new woman.' It would be the slack time of the year, after Christmas, nobody ventured out much because of the bad weather and the depression and illnesses of winter, and there were always so many regular customers still away with relatives and friends, or simply altering the routine by changing towns and hotels. The shop could be closed and no harm done. Mrs Oddicott could then take a holiday in Edinburgh with her niece by marriage, who had so kindly offered last year and been turned down.

'I have heard such a lot about Edinburgh,' Deirdre Fount would say, 'it is an airy, clean and cultured city, full of noble monuments and quality shops, you will be glad of the chance to see everything, a week will scarcely be enough indeed, and I shall have to beg you to come home!' Yes, that is what she would say, she would be firm about it, not allow herself to be dictated to any longer. Her mother should see that she could not always expect to get her own way.

She sat back in the wing chair and rested her head and was suddenly tired with all the making of decisions and resolutions, the effort at clear thinking. The sherry was very soothing and she was no longer alarmed by the idea that her former husband had that day walked into the shop. Aubrey Fount, too, would be dealt with in a calm and natural manner, he would take his son out to tea and they would both get to know one another and enjoy themselves, there would be no hard feelings or awkwardness, and then he would leave Westbourne and all would be as before.

Suddenly, there seemed a great many things to be done and occasions to look forward to. James had to be prepared for the arrival of his father, a place chosen for her holiday and a particularly nice Christmas present bought for Mrs Oddicott. She had to decide what to wear for dinner with the Carpenters at the Prince of Wales Hotel, perhaps even to buy something new. My life has taken a turn for the better, thought Deirdre Fount, it is not hopeless after all. And for the moment I shall not tell my mother about Aubrey's visit, not until all the arrangements for his outing with James have been settled. It will be the same with the holiday, I do not want to leave her any time to defeat me.

Somebody else came into the hotel lounge, and the clock struck half-past six. Now is the moment to return calmly home, she decided, now I feel able to deal with the residue of my mother's anger about this morning.

'Good evening, Mrs Carmichael,' said Deirdre Fount, walking confidently past, 'What a cold evening! So pleasant beside the fire!'

I shall do this again some day, she thought, I have enjoyed my little treat, my rest and my glass of sherry, a quiet time to order my thoughts, it has all done me a great deal of good.

Mrs Carmichael sat reading her library book and waiting for a friend, and when the friend arrived she said at once to her, 'Poor Mrs Fount has just been in here, sitting alone over a glass of sherry.'

Deirdre Fount walked forward into the east wind that blew down the Esplanade. Now is the time, she said to herself, now is the time!

They had begun their evening meal without her.

'Well now!' said Deirdre Fount brightly, walking into the dining room, 'How nice to see a coal fire! I hope you have both left something for me, I am quite ravenous – shall I find it in the oven?'

Mrs Oddicott looked across the table at her grandson.

'If you have quite finished, James, you may go upstairs and get on with your music practice.'

James Fount went without a word. In the dining room there was silence.

'It is really *very* cold out,' said Deirdre Fount at last, and chafed her hands together before the fire, 'there is a very nasty east wind along the sea front, I felt it go straight through to the skin.'

Mrs Winifred Oddicott took a spoonful of greengage jam on to the side of her plate.

'There is some supper for me? But I am quite happy to cook it for myself, you know, mother, whichever may be the case. I thought I could smell shepherd's pie.'

'If it has not altogether dried out at the edges.'

Deirdre Fount went into the kitchen and hummed 'Kelvin Grove' to herself as she lifted dishes out of the oven with a cloth, for she was uneasy, something was going to be said about her rudeness this morning, and her mother would have to be coaxed and humoured for a long time. I must not lose my nerve, she thought, for I have something to say and I intend to say it boldly. Though perhaps it may be best to apologize first, to take all the blame upon myself and find some reasonable excuse for what I said. That will pave the way, and when she has forgiven me we may talk amicably over our coffee in the sitting room.

'In case you were planning to avoid the whole subject,' said Mrs Winifred Oddicott, when her daughter returned, 'or to tell me some lie about it, there is no need, I am quite aware of everything that has been going on.'

'Everything?'

Deirdre Fount looked at the expression on her mother's face. Someone has telephoned, she thought, someone has rung up on some pretext or other and told her that I have just been drinking in the lounge of the Majestic Hotel. Oh, it is too bad! I cannot do anything, I cannot have any privacy, any time to myself in this terrible town where everyone is full of gossip and malice and inquisitiveness. Yet why should I not do precisely as I choose, why am I sitting here with a sense of guilt heavy upon me? I have had my taste of freedom and I will not be intimidated, I am a grown woman. And what is more I plan to take a holiday with my son. I shall speak about it in just a moment.

Mrs Winifred Oddicott was looking at her daughter.

'You are very flushed, Deirdre. And that is scarcely surprising, you have every right to be flushed – with embarrassment and shame.'

'Oh, this is too much!' Deirdre Fount laid her fork down, all appetite gone. 'This is going too far, mother! What have I to be ashamed of? Why should I not enjoy myself a little, once in a while, and spend some time alone and in comfort without first consulting you?'

'If that were true, dear, I should have nothing to say. Indeed, no! What you do alone, in your own time, does not concern me, naturally, it is entirely your own affair. But the truth of the matter is that you have not been alone.'

'Of course I have been alone.'

'I am perfectly well aware,' said Mrs Oddicott, stirring her tea and speaking each word with the greatest care, '*perfectly*, of what has been going on this past hour. I do not miss all that goes on in Westbourne, I keep my eyes open. I too have seen him.'

Deirdre Fount looked up in alarm.

'Aubrey,' said Mrs Winifred Oddicott, 'Aubrey Fount has had the tactlessness to come here to Westbourne. And after all that has happened, after all this time, you have welcomed him, you have not had the good sense or good taste to refuse him a meeting. That is where you have been this evening, and you have thought to keep it from me. Well, once I would have expected better of you, once I would not have been afraid that you would let me down. But now – you have recently been behaving in such a peculiar way that anything might happen, anything. As a daughter you are a disappointment to me, Deirdre, a bitter disappointment. I can only think that you may be unwell and pray that you will come to your senses. It is not,' she rose to her feet, 'not as though you were the only one involved. That is all I have to say.'

Mrs Oddicott walked from the room.

So that is that, thought Deirdre Fount, and that has proved the very last straw. My mind is now quite made up. After suffering such unjust treatment, after being spoken to by my own mother as though I were a naughty little child, I will not be deterred, I will not consider her feelings for she has not considered mine. No one shall stand in my way.

She lifted up the teapot with a shaking hand.

'Oh, it is so nice to hear you, dear, so nice!' said Mrs Flora Carpenter.

'Whoever is this on the telephone, Flora? I want to watch the television news. Tell them that they must say what they have to say quickly or else ring back.'

Mrs Carpenter put her hand over the receiver. 'Just a moment, hold on for a moment ... Bertram, I cannot hear, it is so difficult with the television, if you could just turn it down a little.'

Major Carpenter did not move.

'We are coming to see you, mother,' said Edward Carpenter, at the other end of the telephone line, 'we can manage this weekend, it seems, with a bit of organization, so everything will soon be under control, you will have no need to worry at all.'

'You are coming, dear? I can't hear you very well, the ...'

'WE ARE COMING.'

'Oh, how nice! Oh, that is a relief, Edward, I shall look forward to that so much.'

Major Bertram Carpenter leaned forward to turn up the volume on a speech about rent rebates.

'In time for dinner on the Friday? Look forward to that, mother.'

'Yes, oh yes, Edward, we will expect you then and we can have a nice long evening all together, straight away. Everything is booked and everything will be lovely for you, I had a word with Mr Plumb – you remember Mr Plumb, the manager? About the suite, you know, and it is all arranged. How nice! Oh, I am so looking forward to seeing you.'

'Fifteen pounds each to one million people who are entitled to it,' the voice on the television said.

'*Who* do we look forward to seeing? What is all this about?'

Mrs Flora Carpenter looked about for her spectacles and the skein of lemon-coloured silk.

'Flora?'

'I thought you wanted to listen to the news, dear.'

For now was the time when she must tell him, now that everything was arranged, and she was a little anxious, she needed to consider how best the news might be phrased.

'How splendid!' she said, glancing at the television screen. 'What a good idea, Bertram, that all those poor people should be able to claim £15 off their house rates, and so sleep more easily in their beds at night. What a difference that will make to so many.'

Major Carpenter blew his nose loudly.

'It is all very well for us, Bertram, but we are comfortably off, and do not need to worry. In any case, of course we no longer have rates to pay.'

'Who is coming, Flora?'

'I beg your pardon, dear, I quite lost track of what you . . . Oh, Bertram, do look, there is that awful man with the suspicious face, the actor we are always seeing and you say that he is over-employed, do you remember? And we thought how silly it was last week that he was playing a clergyman and of course it simply did not seem right at all because everyone would remember him as that peculiar doctor who experimented on his patients, and . . .'

'Do not talk to me about doctors,' said Major Bertram Carpenter, and he switched off the television set. 'And let me remind you here and now that if I am in any way ill this winter I do not want to have anything to do with doctors, they are none of them to be trusted.'

'And I have told you that this is a foolish way of talking. They made you better last winter, you would have died of your bronchitis without the assistance of Doctor Rogers.'

'Do not chatter to me about doctors and clergymen in television plays. Flora, you are being deliberately evasive. *Who* do we look forward to seeing here?'

'Edward, dear! Now I am sure you will agree that this is a very pleasant surprise. Edward is coming up for the weekend.'

'Why? What is Edward doing with time on his hands at this time of year? And money on his hands, to pay for a weekend at this hotel. We are always given to understand in the newspapers that house prices are slumping and land is almost unobtainable, that estate agents are finding it hard to make ends meet. But then, Edward always was foolish over money matters, he does not see that he is almost middle-aged and has two boys to provide for, he simply sits back and relies on me, knowing that he will be comfortable the moment I die.'

Mrs Carpenter lowered her head over the stitching.

'It is tactless and inconvenient of them. I am assuming that you did tell them about Isepp?'

'Yes. But we thought that a visit from them would take your mind off things, Bertram, cheer you up a little.'

'Cheer me up? What kind of a man do you take me for, Flora? I am not to be *cheered up* like a convalescent child. My friend Isepp is dead and that is not something I am likely to forget because my son arrives here for the weekend. As for taking my mind off the important matters of life and death – well, it has been off those for too long, Flora, and it has taken the loss of Isepp to bring me to my senses, to make me see what a mockery it is.'

'What is, dear?'

'What is what?'

'A mockery.'

'It is *all* a mockery,' said Major Bertram Carpenter.

'I see.'

'I have been writing a long letter.'

'Yes, dear, I have noticed that.'

'A letter of complaint, a letter of protest, and full of the most detailed facts. They will not get away with it, Flora, though half the public may be content to be bamboozled by all this secrecy and professional jargon. But those doctors did not take sufficient care, they were guilty of negligence and who knows which of us will be the next to suffer at their hands? Isepp should not have died. They talk of giving wonder drugs and exchanging this heart for that, this man's kidney for that man's liver, as though it were all child's play to them, yet my friend Isepp had nothing more than a severe cold and was left to die.'

I will be so very glad to see Edward, thought Mrs Flora Carpenter, Edward will know what to do.

'As long as he doesn't bring that woman with him.'

'Oh, of course he will bring Auriole, what nonsense you talk. Why can you not let bygones be bygones, Bertram? She has been a good wife to him for fifteen years, and if there is something in her manner which does not altogether . . . Well, she is our daughter now, the mother of our grandsons, and it is time you learned to accept her as she is.'

'So she is coming with him, we are to be inflicted with a whole weekend of her, a weekend of useless chatter. I am sorry that you did not see fit to put them off, Flora, it is a most unhappy time.'

'We have not seen them since our return from the cruise.'

'They have always visited us at their own convenience, never at ours.'

Major Carpenter went off into the bedroom and returned wearing his overcoat and the yellow muffler.

'I am taking a walk, Flora.'

'Oh, my dear, but it is gone ten o'clock! There is a bitter wind, do you really think . . .'

But he walked to the door and did not reply and she watched him in tears of anxiety. For a moment, the back of his head reminded her abruptly of how he had once been, in a uniform fifty years ago, so that when he turned round again, she expected to see his face young and with the plump, unlined cheeks, and was shocked at the change, and at seeing the shape of his skull under the crumpled, sallow skin. He is not the same, thought Mrs Carpenter, I do not know him any longer, he is another man. And she wondered just when the change had come over him, when he had ceased to be the young man with the plump and unlined cheeks.

After only a moment, he returned.

'You need not lead them to expect that I shall start buying

them dinners and sending them back home loaded with expensive presents and cheques, Flora. Edward is a grown man, he must make his own way in life, support himself.'

When he had gone out again, Mrs Flora Carpenter wept a little over the lemon-coloured embroidery.

Outside, Major Carpenter leaned on the railings of the Esplanade and looked down into the darkness, towards the wild November sea. I shall not see Isepp again, he thought, never see him again, and one day they will be saying the same of me. We are caught like rats in a trap.

In the bar of the Ship and Castle, Aubrey Fount sat with a whisky and water and his arm around a girl.

'It is a very amazing thing, Yvonne,' he said, 'One of the miracles of life, and when it happens to us we should take notice.'

'It has never happened to me before. But I feel that I can say anything to you, that you understand at once. We *know* one another.'

'There is a rapport, yes. It is almost a chemical reaction set up between us. How amazing that you should have noticed it. I had no idea...'

Aubrey Fount did not finish the sentence, only reached for his glass. The Ship and Castle was small and dimly lit and half-way up the long path that led from the coastguards' cottages on the North Shore. There was no chance that anybody he knew, or who recognized him as a visitor to the Prince of Wales Hotel, would come here. Deirdre Fount and Mrs Oddicott and all the hotel residents were a mile and a half away above the South Bay. He could sit on with his arm about the shoulders of the girl Yvonne, who had come in here and waited over a glass of tomato juice for three quarters of an hour before accepting that it had only been a vague arrangement, and that the man Clifford would not come into the bar now. But I have so little, she had thought, I am not attractive to men and perhaps this was my last chance, nobody else will enter my life. While Aubrey Fount had watched her across the room and been sympathetic when the moment came.

Perhaps it is not so much that I need the company of women, he thought, but that *they* need me. There are so many men who are uneasy with them, do not go about things in the right way, but women feel safe with me, they respond, they all give me their trust and confidence. Although he recognized that he himself found it easier to talk to women than to other men, he felt free to be entirely himself and at the same time, rather more expansive.

'*You* have had it happen to you,' said Yvonne. 'You know what it feels like, I can tell. You have waited for someone who did not come, you have felt let down and belittled, cheated. I can see it in your eyes.'

Aubrey Fount had looked at her tenderly and taken their glasses up to the bar. The girl Yvonne, who was almost thirty-two years old, not really a girl at all, had watched him, her cheeks very flushed.

'You see how much I know about you already,' she said. 'I have only to study your face.'

Aubrey Fount smiled.

'Tell me,' she said, 'whatever there is to tell, all of it. You know that I will understand. You can tell me what you have never been able to tell anyone before.'

'No,' said Aubrey Fount, and he spoke firmly, with resolution that she admired at once. 'No, I do not intend to use you of all people as a shoulder to cry on, I am not going to indulge myself, Yvonne. I could do that if I chose, but I could also do it in any public bar, at any time. I could walk in and buy some man a drink, strike up a conversation and have him stay and listen to me, I could pour out my troubles to a sympathetic barmaid. The country is full of men who make a habit of that sort of behaviour, it is too easy for them. But I will not be like that, and certainly not with you. We have only just met but our relationship is much too important.'

'Yes, oh, I feel that too,' said the girl Yvonne. 'How moving that you should say so to me, Aubrey!'

The man Clifford from the Borough Engineer's Department, upon whom she had for so long pinned all her hopes, and who did not care and might have met her here this evening or might not, who was kind and vague about their friendship and had never so much as held her hand, that man faded out of her mind, and she looked at Aubrey Fount in amazement.

This is how it happens to other people, she thought, and now it has happened to me, I have pictured it all and yet I could never have pictured the reality, I have dreamed about it but never believed. Women in magazines and books and the cinema meet strange men with whom they feel an instant excitement and understanding but I am not that sort of woman. Here is a man who *needs* me, a man I feel I can look after and care for and strengthen, a tired, honest, sorrowing man. I am thirty-two years old and I have been waiting all my life for this, and if he had come to me when I was younger and more confident and self-assured, then I would never have recognized him.

'There is one thing that I do not like to think of, but think of it I must,' said Aubrey Fount now, and laid his hand over hers. She is plain, he thought, plain and intense but soft-fleshed and not without promise. 'When I think that I almost cancelled this trip altogether – I did not want to take a holiday alone, I almost carried right on working because there seemed to be no point in anything else and work is the best alcohol, Yvonne, the best cure for many ills.'

'You were lonely,' said Yvonne. 'You were going to tire yourself out with work, in order to forget.'

Aubrey Fount looked down into his glass. 'Do not let us think about it,' he said.

'About?'

'I am not here in Westbourne for very long. I have only just met you and we do not have much time to be together.'

Yvonne's hand moved under his. 'You will go away,' she said in a dull voice, 'that will be the end of it, I know. It is all too sudden, and too good to be true, I am expecting more to happen than can *possibly* happen. You will get home and forget all about me, someone else will soon be there. Oh, I can feel it! You will go away.'

'My dear girl,' said Aubrey Fount, and his voice was rather serious now, rather quiet, 'My dear Yvonne, what kind of a man do you take me for? I only want you to have your eyes open, to understand that there are so many complications in my life. I do not want to burden you with any of it, though some day you will have to know – to know a little at least. But whatever difficulties and problems I have are not to be discussed now, I will not have this evening spoiled, and you will never be troubled by them in any way. What matters is that I have met you, that we know at once there is something between us.'

For some moments they were silent. Two men came into the bar suddenly, and beyond the open door came the sound of wind and sea crashing together.

I shall have to be careful what I say, thought Aubrey Fount, perhaps I have already gone too far, for the sake of an evening or so of female company.

'Yvonne,' he said, 'I should tell you, I have not always . . .'

Yvonne interrupted him. 'Do not say anything, do not begin to tell me about yourself or to make any confessions, do not talk about doubts and problems. We have all of us something in the past of which we cannot be proud and which we regret later. But I can see that you are a good person, Aubrey, I know you already. Only three hours ago I did not know that you existed and now all this has happened between us. I do not believe that I am deceived in any way at all.'

'Yes, yes, you are right, Yvonne, there is no use in talking of problems. This does not happen every day, we should make the best of it.'

And he allowed his hand to slip a little lower so that it almost lay against her breast.

'Aubrey,' said the girl Yvonne, 'I should tell you at once, dear, I do not . . .'

Aubrey Fount put up his finger and touched her rather pale mouth. 'No, no, do not tell *me* anything either. I only want to *know* you. Yvonne. You must trust me.'

'Very well. I trust you, Aubrey.'

Good God, thought Aubrey Fount, what am I encouraging this girl to think and say?

He drank up the last of his whisky and thought of Miriam.

Why, it is easy, said Deirdre Fount, and laughed at herself as she walked up Lime Avenue. She had simply said, at a quarter to four, 'I will leave you now, mother, you can hold the fort until it is time to close, I think.'

Mrs Winifred Oddicott, who had scarcely spoken since the previous evening, except when words could not be avoided, said now, 'You are going to meet that man, you have no shame, but I am ashamed for you.'

'No. I am going to meet James from school. Perhaps I am taking your advice for once! There is something important I have to say to him.'

She had combed her hair and put on some lipstick and buttoned up her coat and walked out, simply *walked out*, and quite cheerfully, too, saying, 'We shall not be very late home,' and not waiting to hear whatever might be her mother's reply.

I should have taken my courage into my hands a long time ago, she said now, as she waited under the bare trees, the huge horse-chestnut and sycamore at the entrance to Westbourne Priors School.

Rather to her own surprise, she had slept well, and in the morning she had not been depressed at all, the events of the previous day now seemed to be landmarks. The tide had turned, thought Deirdre Fount, and I shall not be left standing on the shore, I am a new woman, I see my opportunities and I shall grasp them with both hands. With such remarks she had comforted herself all day, in the face of her mother's scorn and disapproval, so that now, at four o'clock, she was quite elated, she felt that she stood a head taller than before.

'Now there you are, James! Isn't this a surprise?'

'Oh,' said James Fount, and stopped dead in the middle of the group of boys with whom he had come out. They walked on, parting around him like water round an island.

'Hello.'

'Do up the belt of your gabardine, dear, it does not look at all nice like that.'

James Fount set down his flute case and satchel carefully on the ground and did as she asked him without a word. He was eleven years old and filled with shame that he should be met from school, even once only, by a mother whose hair frizzed up in the rain and who told him loudly about the belt of his gabardine. He was surprised, too, for it was not like her, it was always his grandmother who said things of that kind.

A bunch of the smaller boys, in their scarlet and grey, passed down the drive and many got into waiting cars. Perhaps that would have been all right, being met by your mother in a *car* was a different matter.

'We are going out to tea, darling, that is why I wanted you to look a little more tidy. You should be proud of your uniform and make the best of yourself in it when you go out in public.'

James Fount picked up his flute case. 'Who are we going out to tea with?' he asked her.

'Why, with one another! We will walk down Victoria Road to the Art Gallery because there is a new exhibition of work by Marine Artists – now do you know what that means?'

James Fount supposed it was inevitable that his mother would come, sooner or later, to be exactly like Mrs Oddicott, that she would grow more like her in more ways than in voice.

'They paint the sea,' he said.

'Yes, of course they do. Watercolours of ships and seascapes and boatyards and beaches, too, all that sort of thing. You will enjoy it.'

James Fount dragged his satchel further up on to his shoulder.

I wonder if all eleven-year-old boys are the same, thought Mrs Fount, if they are difficult and uncommunicative. I do not know any of his friends, they never come to the house and so I have had no experience. But perhaps it is because he has no father, his background may now be telling against him.

'Quiet', 'A satisfactory worker', 'Co-operative', 'A responsible member of the form', 'Shows interest', were the sort of things his reports always said, and they all seemed to be pleased with him, the headmaster had never asked to see her in order to complain and so she had never been really worried.

'You would not like a rude, noisy boy,' Mrs Winifred Oddicott had often told her, 'James has a placid, serious nature, though he is a little highly strung. But I am sure he knows how to let off steam on the right occasions.'

'A competent half-back,' the reports also said. 'Bowls with accuracy.'

And so perhaps it *was* all right.

The tea room of the Art Gallery was warm and lit with satin-shaded lamps on individual tables. There was a rose-patterned carpet and Masons china, the smell of toasted tea-cakes and steam. James Fount looked politely at the marine watercolours and drawings and oils and sculpture, and then at the permanent collection, portraits of local dignitaries after 1800, with robes and chains and heavy, well-fed faces. From time to time, Deirdre Fount would say, Oh, *this* is very good, James, and, Do you like that one, dear?

'We could have gone to the museum,' said James Fount, 'and looked at the butterflies in cases.'

The museum was next door.

'Oh, but it always smells so in there, dear, so fusty and cold, and besides, there is not tea.' And so they went on, walking in and out of the picture rooms until they had seen all and they could eat.

'Toasted buns, I think,' said Deirdre Fount, 'and tomato sandwiches and cake. I know what an appetite you have when you come from school! Isn't this a treat, now? I never have you to myself these days.'

James Fount looked out of the bay windows on to the tops of the elm trees.

'There are rooks' nests,' he said, 'you can see right into them.'

'Yes.'

'In a minute it will be dark.'

At another table, two clergymen ate muffins and the butter ran down their chins.

'Schwartz has got a model of the Flying Scotsman,' said James Fount, 'it's new, it cost five pounds. He said I could go and look at it.'

'How nice! James dear, I brought you here so that we could have a talk together. Something quite important has happened this week – more important for you than for me. Now I wonder how I can best explain it to you.'

How like his father he is, she thought again, for she had noticed it at once after she had seen Aubrey the previous day. The light shone on the reddish glints in her son's bushy hair and there was something about the eyes, too, though thank goodness he had none of Aubrey's weakness of lower lip and chin, the boy's features were all firm and well-spaced.

Perhaps I am to leave school, thought James Fount, and be sent away, perhaps someone has died and left money and I can go to be a boarder. He had often wished for it, to go away and board at a school, and learn to be a very good flute player indeed, that seemed to be his only chance.

To help her on, therefore, he said aloud, 'Westbourne Priors is all *right*, but it isn't . . . it isn't everything, you know.'

'Oh!' said Deirdre Fount startled, and the words she had carefully arranged together in her mind were dispersed at once, she could not begin. He is going to tell me that he is unhappy at school, she thought, and I can do nothing at all about it. Oh . . .

'No, dear,' she said, 'I suppose not. But you . . .'

At that moment, the tea came.

Chapter Seven

DEAR MRS FOUNT (the letter read),

I am very sorry indeed to have to write this little note to cancel our invitation of last week. But a very close friend of my husband has recently died and it has *so* shocked us both – indeed, Bertram is quite ill.

Under the circumstances I feel we cannot give a dinner party just yet and give our guests all the attention and entertainment we would wish. It would have been so very nice to see you, but we do hope you will forgive us, and that, when things are better, we may confidently expect to have the pleasure of your company one evening.

Yours ever,
Flora Carpenter

Oh, said Deirdre Fount, and then hid the envelope quickly under a petticoat in her dresser drawer, for there was a footstep on the stairs. Oh, that is a disappointment to me! For the scene in the red and gold dining room of the Prince of Wales Hotel, with its chandeliers and bevelled mirrors and trolleys loaded with every kind of exotic sweet, had danced before her mind's eye.

But there will be another occasion, of course, as Mrs Carpenter has said, I will still have it to look forward to. And meanwhile, I will not let this spoil my enjoyment in this newfound freedom. There will be Christmas, and then our holiday. Tomorrow, she had decided to go into the public library and spend a long time looking over brochures and lists of hotels. Then, she could surprise James with a second piece of news, and tell her mother very firmly what arrangements she had made.

Tonight, however, she was to telephone to Aubrey about his outing with James. Or perhaps, she thought, perhaps I could go there, to the Prince of Wales Hotel, and he will buy me a drink or some coffee and I can say a quick and comforting word to the Carpenters. Yes, it will make a nice evening out.

Deirdre Fount began to look through her wardrobe, deciding what would be suitable to wear.

'Mr Fount does not appear to be in his room, Madam.'

'Oh? Oh, well . . .'

'I will have him paged for you.'

'Oh, no! No, there is really no need, I could just go and look myself . . .'

But the reception clerk had pressed the bell and a boy came at once, so that Deirdre Fount felt herself caught up in the official machinery of the hotel and dared not protest. She did not feel at home here as she had felt in the lounge of the Majestic Hotel, she felt alarmed and overawed, thinking that everyone would notice if she behaved incorrectly or was at all unsuitably dressed.

'If you would care to take a seat, Madam?'

Beyond the lobby she could see a ballroom, with men in dinner jackets and a microphone on a gilded dais.

'Paging Mr Aubrey Fount, please, paging Mr Aubrey Fount . . .'

Oh, what am I doing here, she thought suddenly? How could I have been so foolish, for he will draw all kinds of wrong conclusions, I shall never dare to meet his eyes.

And then she saw Major Carpenter walking towards her down the staircase, and she got up with relief, feeling more comfortable at once because she was able to claim acquaintance with a resident, stand talking and show that she belonged here.

'Major Carpenter! How very nice . . . I am so pleased for I was hoping to have a word with one of you, while I was in the hotel.'

Major Bertram Carpenter stopped at the foot of the staircase and frowned. He looks old, thought Deirdre Fount, the skin below his eyes is pouched and stained, he has suffered a bad shock.

'How are you?' she asked him, stepping forward, and laying a hand momentarily on his arm, 'I was so sorry to hear about your sad loss. If there is anything I can do for you . . .'

He will go up and tell his wife, she thought, and Mrs Carpenter will then come downstairs, or else I will be invited to their suite for coffee, perhaps even a liqueur. The Carpenters were important residents.

But Major Carpenter stared at her, and his eyes were vacant, he twitched a little in order to brush her hand from off his sleeve.

'Perhaps your wife is here?' said Deirdre Fount hurriedly, 'I would so like to speak to her if she has a spare moment . . .'

She was afraid that Aubrey would appear suddenly from one of the side lounges and march up to her, demand to be introduced and cause her a great deal of embarrassment.

'Madam,' said Major Bertram Carpenter, 'I have quite forgotten your name.'

'I am Mrs Fount,' she said, puzzled and also rather affronted. 'Mrs Deirdre Fount.'

'Mrs Fount, from the draper's shop?'

She flushed. How demeaning, she thought, and how like a man to mark her off in that impolite way. Mrs Fount the shopkeeper, and therefore someone of no account, scarcely a person in her own right.

'I would be glad to know, Mrs Fount, how *you* have heard what you call my sad loss? To what exactly are you referring? Let us be quite clear.'

'A close friend of yours has died, I understand.'

'You knew Mr Isepp?'

'Oh not at all, I'm afraid.'

'I have not gone about the town saying that a close friend of mine has died, it is not the sort of thing one gossips about. But someone has gossiped and you have heard them in your shop.'

'I am not in the habit of listening to gossip, Major Carpenter, I do assure you. No, your wife wrote to me and told me about your friend and that is why I have spoken to you about it. It is only courteous to offer sympathy in such cases, but if I have offended . . .'

'My *wife* wrote to you?'

'Of course.'

There was a footstep behind Deirdre Fount and she turned round quickly, wondering if she could get away, and avoid introducing Aubrey to Major Carpenter. She wanted to be done with this embarrassing conversation.

'Mr Fount does not appear to be in the hotel anywhere, Madam. If you would care to leave a message for him at the desk?'

'Oh, no. No thank you, that is quite all right. Thank you for your trouble, but I will not leave any message.'

When she turned around again, Major Carpenter was gone. Deirdre Fount fled from the hotel.

In the back of the six-seater American saloon, parked by a hedge beyond the golf links, Aubrey Fount muttered to the girl Yvonne, breathing hard, and the rain drummed down upon the car roof.

'You are doing remarkably well,' said Mr Ralph Porlock.

James Fount looked up in surprise, his face flushed. Praise was very rarely forthcoming, there would only be a nod of the head, a grunt, 'That will do', at the end of a piece.

'Thank you,' he said, and began to take his flute carefully apart and wipe out the moisture.

'Grade Six,' said Mr Porlock, 'in March.'

'Oh. Oh, but I haven't done Five yet.'

'I think you need not.'

Porlock went to the cabinet and took out his bottle of ale. 'Play the Mozart a little more slowly,' he said, ripping off the metal cap, 'but it needs to be *spry*, you know – *ta*-ta-ta, *ta*-ta-ta, *ta*-two-three . . .' and he snapped his fingers in the air. 'How is your grandmother?'

James Fount looked down into his music case and muttered. He would never forgive her for what she had done by coming here, though she had never mentioned it to him. He had wanted to run somewhere and bury his face and scream for humiliation and rage when Porlock had told him, laughing and laughing.

'Oh, don't worry, boy, never *worry*,' he said now.

James Fount watched him drink the beer. The froth stayed in a pale rim around his mouth.

'I wondered . . .'

Mr Porlock looked over the top of his glass.

'You see, it's my father.'

'Father? *Have* you a father?'

'Yes. I have now. He turned up.'

'From where?'

'I don't know. Wherever he lives. He has been to see my mother.'

'And do you find him satisfactory, is he what you expect a father to be?'

'I haven't seen him, yet. Only mother has seen him. I don't know what to expect.'

'Probably a good thing – whatever you expected would be wrong. Do you see?'

'Oh.'

Porlock looked at the boy. How stiff he is and how uncertain, he thought, how afraid he is of being himself and of giving anything away. Perhaps a father is just what he needs.

'Is he come to stay here?'

'Oh no, it's just a visit. I think he will take me out. I don't know why he should have come – would you know why?' He turned anxiously.

'No,' said Mr Ralph Porlock, and went to stand over by the window. He touched a globe lightly with his finger, turning it from side to side. The world is a very satisfying shape, he had once said, and James Fount had been puzzled and not known how to reply. He had not thought of the shape of the world, or whether it might be good or bad, but ever since then, he had felt comforted because the master had said it was 'satisfying'.

'I have to choose,' he said now. 'My father will come to meet me out of school and I can choose where I want to go. But I don't know where to say.'

'Good heavens, there ought to be any number of things you want to do, plenty of places you can find to go.'

'Yes. I suppose so.'

'But?'

'I don't know.'

'There is no use asking me, Fount, I have no idea where you should go. Why should I have any idea?'

'I thought you might. Never mind.'

James Fount picked up his flute case, feeling disappointed. 'I'll go now,' he said.

Poor little devil, thought Ralph Porlock, poor little devil, with that grandmother and a father who turns up out of the blue and takes him out to tea.

'It would be better if it was summer, we could go to the amusement park or on a speedboat. I've never been on a speedboat. But there's nothing much in the winter.'

'At tea-time in the Majestic Hotel,' said Mr Porlock solemnly, 'they play selections from musical comedies. "The Desert Song", "No, No, Nanette" and so forth. The Roy Robson Trio.'

'Not in winter.'

'Ah.'

'I don't think I should like that very much, anyway.'

'No. I do not think that you would.'

'If it weren't too late for conkers we could have gone in the park.'

'It is always too late for something in this life,' said Ralph Porlock, and was depressed, because it was so easy to impress schoolboys with such remarks, it was so very easy to appear wise.

'Well, ask for a tea somewhere,' he said from the doorstep, 'a good big tea. Be on the safe side.'

James Fount nodded, and walked away from him down the drive.

'Are you safe, Fount? Alone on the cliff path?'

The boy looked back over his shoulder with an expressionless face.

Poor little devil, Porlock thought again, closing the door, and went to open a tin of sardines for himself, before the arrival of the next pupil. I am content with my life, he said, I have all I require. I am luckier than most.

Though he had wondered, lately, if that were true.

James Fount began to run down the path.

'There's a programme about Great Western Steam,' Schwartz had said that afternoon. They were in the sports hut, pulling off shirts and untying bootlaces, everyone steaming and sweating. James Fount had looked up at once.

'Eight o'clock, don't forget to watch it.'

'We don't have a television, do we? How can I?'

'Heck! Oh well, come and watch ours then, that'll be all right.'

'Oh.'

'Then you could see the Flying Scotsman as well.'

'I'd have to ask.'

Schwartz lived on the other side of the park. His father was a dentist.

'You could come to tea if you like,' he said.

'No, because of my flute lesson.'

'Well, come after. Come as soon as you can.'

'I'm not sure.'

'Why not? It'll be great. You don't want to miss it, do you?'

'No, only I have to ask, that's all, because of buses and things.'

'Well, my father will take you home, won't he?'

'Oh.'

'Of course. And it's a Seventeen to Denham Avenue, from the Clock, to get there.'

'But your mother doesn't know.'

'Oh, that's all right, people are always just coming, she never minds.'

Schwartz had walked away, whistling, towards the shower.

James Fount ran all the way home through the cold streets, his breath panting out in front of him like smoke. To go to Schwartz's house, to be with his family watching their television, surrounded by their furniture, seemed the most desirable activity he could think of. Schwartz might become his own friend.

He slowed down and began to walk very carefully along the street, for he might trip and break his leg or slip on wet leaves and fall under the wheels of a car, and then he would not be able to go.

He began to call out the moment he pushed open the front door. 'Mother? Mother where are you? Are you upstairs? There's something I've got to ask you and it's important. Mother!'

In the sitting room the electric fire glowed red and made a soft whirring sound but nobody sat there and the dining room was still in darkness. He burst into the kitchen, impatient to ask and be gone again, to wait for the number seventeen bus by the Clock Tower.

Mrs Winifred Oddicott sat at the kitchen table, snuffling into a handkerchief. The lid of the electric kettle was rattling up and down as the water boiled away inside.

'Where's my mother? Has she gone upstairs?'

'No.'

'Oh. Oh, well ...'

Mrs Oddicott sniffed and blew her nose hard. Her eyes were red, and in order not to have to look at her, or ask what had happened, James Fount went to the refrigerator and poured himself a glass of milk.

'She has gone out, gone off once again.'

He drank the milk uneasily.

'And I suppose it does not dawn on *you* to lift a hand and switch off the kettle, I suppose I am expected to get up and do that as I do everything for both of you in this house.'

He moved forward hastily and flicked down the switch.

'If you are going to ask me where she has gone, it is of no use, I cannot tell you. *I* have not been informed.'

'It doesn't matter. Can I go and watch television at Schwartz's house? It's only a seventeen bus from the Clock and they'll bring me back in their car, I wouldn't be late. Will that be all right?'

'I am sure *I* do not know what you may or may not do, I am not the one to say. I must take a back seat where you are concerned, or so I have just been told. I am only your grandmother, though what would have happened to you without me, I dare not think, and who else would be here to see to you at times like this, when your mother is not here? She gets up, puts on her coat and walks out of that front door no sooner than she has come in and does not so much as say where she is going, or when she will be back. Not a word has been said to me and do not ask me about it.'

'But I need to know, I want to go. They said any time, I can go straight away, if it's all right.'

'You are all alike, you think only of yourselves, never of me. You will go out, and when you are older you will go off somewhere, you will turn out to be just like your father and *that* will not be anything to be proud of, let me tell you. You are old enough to know these things, I have kept silent long enough. And now *I* am told to pack my bags and be off somewhere, to the house of strangers miles away and in the depths of winter, just so that the two of *you* may go off on a holiday together. Oh, and I am told quite casually about it, too, when all arrangements have been made, and it seems that I have no choice in the matter. Well, I daresay it was only to be expected, I should have recognized the truth of things long ago.'

Oh, be quiet, be quiet, thought James Fount, as he stood by the gas cooker, clenching and unclenching his hands and hot with embarrassment. I do not want to hear, you shouldn't say any of it to me. He wanted to race outside or stop his eyes and ears so that he could not hear the tearful voice complaining on and on. It is not my fault, he would have said, how can I help what other people do or what my mother may have said?

'*Can* I go? It will be all right, really.'

'Have I not already told you, do not ask me, I am of no account, I am not the one to say.'

'But you can say, you always have, and I won't be late or anything. It's not *far*.'

Mrs Winifred Oddicott turned around and raised her voice hysterically, so that he took a quick step backwards, in alarm.

'Very well, go then, go where you like, do not think of me left alone here. You are every bit as bad as they are, and I am sure I do not care what you do, you are no longer any concern of mine.'

James Fount went, although the evening was spoiled now, there was a sick feeling in the pit of his stomach. Nothing could be taken for granted any longer, things were not going to be the same.

Ten minutes later, coming in from her walk to the pillar box, Deirdre Fount said, 'Ah, there is James's flute case – so he has come home?'

I will not let her get me down, she had decided earlier, I will not respond to her provocation, I shall be as usual; calm and quiet and amiable, and she must come round when she chooses.

'Has he gone to his room?'

Mrs Oddicott lifted the lid of a saucepan and peered inside. 'He is gone out,' she said shortly.

'Out? Out where? He did not tell me of any plan he had to go out again.'

'And is that not only to be expected? He is taking after you in that respect, surely.'

'Mother, do not be ridiculous. Where has he gone?'

'Now I suppose I am to be blamed for giving permission. But what else was I supposed to do? You were not here, and I made it very clear that I was no longer thought to be responsible for him, I said all that there was to say on that score. James knows all that has happened.'

'Mother ...'

'He has gone to the house of a friend, that was the story.'

'What friend?'

'To watch a television set.'

'*What* friend?'

'A foreign name. Schwepp or Schmidt, I really do not remember.'

'Schwartz?'

'It may have been.'

'Mark Schwartz. His father is Schwartz the dentist.'

Mrs Oddicott poured water from the pan of cauliflower and clouds of steam rose up around her.

'Well, it is too bad of him to have gone off like that, I would never have allowed it at such short notice, and certainly not without making sure about the arrangements. He is not an adult, he is only eleven years old.'

'Are they to bring him home?'

'Really, Deirdre, it is of no use asking me, you must – as you yourself said – take more responsibility for your own son, play a major part in his life. That was what you decided, and so I am afraid I think it is your duty to find out about all these little matters, not mine.'

'Mother, you are being very trying indeed, I am finding it very hard to keep my temper.'

'Oh, do not keep it on my account!'

'How could I find anything out, when I was not here to ask?'

'Precisely!'

'Dear God, I only went to the end of the road, to post a letter!'

'But *I* did not know that, I could not tell him to wait a few minutes, until you came back, for I did not know when you would be back. If I have taken too much upon my own shoulders I am sure I apologize, Deirdre, it will not happen in the future, I do assure you. I intend to think of myself just a little more, to live my own life and leave you, as you have requested, to be in complete charge of yours.'

'There is no need to take that attitude, no need to be childish and take offence at the slightest thing. It is all because I have told you about my plans for the holiday, that is why I am having this now.'

'It is you who have brought *that* subject up again, please note. *I* have said nothing at all about it.'

'And am I expected to tell you my every movement? Can I not so much as go out to post a letter . . .?'

'Oh, pardon me! You manage not only to go out and post letters, you go here and there without ever having the courtesy to inform me when you leave the house. You are a law unto yourself, you do not like to tell me of your movements, yet I am expected to be here the whole time, and to stand in for you on all occasions. You are only able to carry on in this selfish way because I am here. Well, do not rely upon that, do not take it for granted, Deirdre. I may not always be here, one day you may be left alone. Yes, indeed!'

Deirdre Fount held her breath and walked from the kitchen. I *will* not allow her to get the better of me, she thought, I will not submit to this moral blackmail, nor will I lose my temper, for that is what she is trying to make me do and then the fault and blame will be all mine.

She began to look through the telephone directory for the name of Schwartz.

'Would you like to play a game of "Scrabble", dear?' asked Mrs Christie, companion to the rich Miss Violet Prug.

'No, thank you.'

'You would prefer Piquet, I daresay. I'll just get the cards.'

'No, I would rather not play Piquet.'

'Oh? Draughts, then? We have not played draughts for many a long day. I am sure I do not mind which.'

Really, thought Miss Prug, it is *you* who need a companion, you are the one who is quite at a loss during these long winter evenings, unless there is some game to be played. She herself was happily enjoying the Regency Bath of *Heir to Lord*

Romney's Fortune. She did not intend to set aside her pleasure.

'Which shall it be, now?' asked Mrs Christie.

'It is very good of you, but at the moment, you see, I am quite content to be reading my book.'

'Oh,' said Mrs Christie. 'Oh.' And stood fidgeting with the handle of the drawer in which the games were kept.

'Why do you not try that new jigsaw? Edinburgh Castle, I think. That would keep you busy.'

'Oh, I can always find plenty to *do*,' said Mrs Christie, a little offended. On a rug in front of the fire, the pekinese dog, Knox, twitched and snuffled its way through a dream.

'Well, I suppose I shall have to play myself at clock patience.'

'Yes. What a good idea!'

Mrs Christie began to fuss and cluck about bringing up the card table and setting it out and finding extra cushions for her chair. In Bath, Miss Prug's heart leaped with that of her heroine at the glad and unexpected sight of Robert Romney in the Pump Rooms.

'Now isn't this cosy?' said Mrs Christie, setting the cards down one by one, flip flip flip on to the polished surface. 'There is something about winter evenings, when we are shut in and sheltered behind doors and curtains, in front of a lovely fire, something so relaxing, I always think.'

Miss Violet Prug, amiable as well as rich, was used to closing her ears to the chatter which Mrs Christie felt it her duty as a companion to provide, while making little random murmurs of comment and interest. 'Hm,' she said now, looking across the Pump Rooms into the dark eyes of Robert Romney.

'*Very* cosy,' said Mrs Christie.

They both started at the sudden peal on the doorbell.

In Denham Avenue, on the other side of the park, James Fount sat in front of a colour television set in the Schwartz living room and drank a strawberry milk shake and thought that he might never be so happy in his life again.

This is the sort of house to live in, he thought, glancing round in the half-darkness, this is the sort of family to have, a proper family. I wish I were Schwartz.

'Have a chocolate biscuit, James,' said Schwartz's mother,

who cared less about teeth, for all her husband was a dentist, than Mrs Fount and Mrs Oddicott together.

James Fount ate and drank and forgot about the anxiety of tomorrow and having to meet an unknown father.

'Oh, perhaps *you* will think it nothing, you will not understand at all, but everything suddenly became too much for me, and I felt that I simply must go out for a change of scene, a breath of fresh air, some different faces,' said Mrs Flora Carpenter.

'Yes, yes, and to have someone listen to you sympathetically, of course that is only natural,' said the rich Miss Prug. 'You have had a good deal to bear, that is clear, and I *do* understand. It is time you shared and halved your troubles.'

In the kitchenette, Mrs Christie set up a tray of coffee and sliced cherry cake.

'He has suffered such a shock, you see, he is beside himself over this death. I should not complain, for it is not altogether his fault that he behaves in this way.'

'Mr Isepp was a very old friend?'

'No. No, I had never realized – they did not seem so very close, but I must not have understood. Men are different, I suppose, men are different.'

Mrs Carpenter stroked the stomach of the Pekinese dog, her face pale with worry and doubt.

'Yes,' said Miss Prug, who had no real idea about whether men were different or not. 'Yes, of course.'

'I am only thankful that Edward can come. Edward will be a tower of strength, he knows what to do for the best on all occasions.'

Miss Prug wondered exactly what could be done in such a situation, but only said, 'And after your lovely holiday, too – it is all a great pity.'

'Oh, the holiday seems a lifetime away, I had almost forgotten it. My husband is a different person, Miss Prug, simply a different person.'

The dog Knox rolled abruptly out of Mrs Carpenter's reach, so that she sat forward, her hand dangling purposelessly over the edge of the chair.

'But just this evening I was so alarmed, for he turned on me, there is no other word for it, he really became quite unpleasant. He accused me of gossiping and being malicious, of having no heart for his grief and the death of his friend, of being disrespectful. But you know how careful I am, you know that I never bear any ill will, Miss Prug, so how *can* any of that be true.'

'No, no, of course not. You must not upset yourself.'

'Bertram has always been such a kind man, a gentle man. Oh, of course he has an impatient streak, especially in times of illness – but who has not?'

'As you say, dear, he is not quite himself just now, and perhaps this is almost a time of illness. He will not be quite aware of what he is saying to you – you must make allowances.'

'I do try,' said Mrs Flora Carpenter, her eyes filling with tears, 'I do try.'

'Now why do you not show the letter to him. That will surely set his mind at rest, it will prove that you said only what needed to be said, in order to cancel the dinner party.'

'But I did not keep a copy, and I am sure Mrs Fount has not, and in any case, I really could not bring myself to ask her.'

'There is no need to ask Mrs Fount. *I* have the letter, do not forget that you sent one to me, too.'

'Of course!'

'Was it the same letter?'

'Oh yes. You see I thought it all out so carefully, once I had seen that the dinner would have to be cancelled. It took me a very long time to compose, because I wanted it to be just right. I would not have offended anyone.'

'Well, you did not. *I* was certainly not offended, I understood perfectly.'

'How kind!'

'Mrs Christie shall look in my writing case and find the letter, and all shall be well.'

'But I do not see how it will do any good, Miss Prug. For you see, Bertram's memory has become so vague and his mind wanders so, that he does not believe any dinner party was planned, after discussion and with his consent. He has no recollection of it. "You are lying, Flora," that is what he said to me,

"You have made these arrangements for your own pleasure, do not try to involve *me*, do not lay the blame at my door, for *I* never wanted any dinner party." That is what he has said. I am ashamed to have to tell you about it.'

'Now do not be upset. Grief and shock take people in strange ways, and perhaps after some rest and when he has seen your son, things may improve no end. Time is the great healer.'

'Yes,' said Mrs Flora Carpenter. 'Yes.' And because she feared to bore Miss Prug, she dried her eyes and smiled, as Mrs Christie entered with the trolley.

'Tell me,' said Violet Prug, pulling the rug up further on to her knees, 'how are those two grandsons of yours? Are they coming with their parents for the weekend?'

Mrs Carpenter sat up straight and began to talk of Charles and Jonathan, and after a little while, she felt better.

James Fount was driven home from Denham Avenue by Mr Schwartz, the dentist, in a silver-grey Rover, and when they came to his own house, he was filled with shame, because it looked so small.

'Come again,' said Mr Schwartz, waving his hand, 'enjoyed having you, come again.'

Mrs Deirdre Fount appeared at the front door in time to be impressed by the departing car.

'I do not think I am at all pleased with you, James, it was very wrong of you not to have told me where you were going.'

'I told grandmother,' said James Fount, and went quickly towards the stairs, not wanting to be asked questions about his evening with Schwartz but to go away and think about it all over and over again, in his own room.

'*I* am your mother, you should have told me.'

'Grandmother said I could go – it's just the same.'

'Oh, no,' said Deirdre Fount, setting her mouth in a hard line. 'No, it is not. In future you will always ask permission of *me*. I am the one who should be responsible for you.'

In the sitting room, Mrs Winifred Oddicott sat listening to every word, as was intended, and her face was also set in a hard expression.

James Fount went up to his own room in silence.

Chapter Eight

'YOUR father will collect you from school,' Mrs Deirdre Fount had said, 'make sure and look out for his car.'

'What kind of car?'

'Oh, I'm afraid I have no idea, James, I forgot to ask. Still, I expect you will know him.'

'Why?'

'Well – well, he will be a man by himself, and you will be able to see that he is not one of the other parents, won't you? You know them.'

'Not all of them. Only a few.'

'Don't be difficult, James.'

'What colour of car is it, then?'

'I really do not – Oh! Wait a minute – Yes, I do, yes – I think I remember, he said it was a white car. There now, that makes it a lot easier, doesn't it?'

'There are a lot of white cars,' said James Fount.

So there were, but none like this. He had been prepared for anything, but not for the huge white American saloon, taking up the kerb space of four minis.

James Fount stopped. That is my father, he thought, and he grew suddenly afraid at what he would have to say and do, what might be expected of him.

'Come on, Fount, walking along?'

A boy, Douglas Macdonald, swung his satchel into the small of James Fount's back.

'No. I'm not going home. I'm going out. With my father. That's my father, there, waiting for me.' He pointed to the American car.

'Oh,' said Douglas Macdonald, 'O.K. then,' and went off swinging his satchel, not looking at the car or being impressed, as was expected of him.

The man at the wheel of the car was looking up, watching every boy closely as they came down the drive. He had ginger hair and a ginger moustache. Then his eye caught that of the boy who stood and stared at him.

He knows, thought James Fount, he knows who I am. He walked slowly forward.

'They will have met, they will be together by now,' said Mrs Deirdre Fount, glancing at her watch. 'Oh, I do so hope everything goes well.'

Mrs Winifred Oddicott, who was checking shades of tapestry wool against the chart, did not speak. It is your affair entirely, she had said to her daughter earlier, I wash my hands of you all, I have no comment to make. But she did not approve, she had made that very clear, she thought that nothing but harm could come of the visit of Aubrey Fount. The boy would now be deeply unsettled.

I will not let any of it upset me, thought Deirdre Fount. I am quite sure in my own mind that this is the right thing to do. Though the ill-feeling between them, the way her mother tightened her lips and turned her head away and refused to speak, the *atmosphere*, did upset her, there was no doubt of it, she had been off her food and waking in the small hours of every morning, to lie and worry. For she is my mother, after all, and unkindness between relatives is always so much worse than between those who are only friends.

For the past two weeks, nothing had been the same. She was uncertain of herself again, she could no longer rely upon her own emotions and ideas, she was unsettled and anxious, determined that the rest of her life should not go to waste but afraid, too, full of misgivings. Aubrey Fount had come to Westbourne, bringing the past with him; she had hoped that it was all done with and now she was forced to meet him again, and remember.

'I will make a cup of tea,' she said, for it would occupy her, and pass the time while James was with his father. 'The shop is very quiet today. I wonder why.'

Mrs Oddicott sniffed.

'Why do you think, mother? The weather is not very good, I suppose – people do not like to venture out in the cold.'

'Oh, I do not think it has much to do with the *weather*. But I will keep my opinions to myself.' And she wrote down 'One Dozen Bermuda Beige, No 090' on the reminder pad for orders.

'Now, whatever is that supposed to mean? I wish you would not make these little knowing remarks, mother, and then expect me to understand them. I am not a mind reader. It is most irritating.'

'You find a great many things that I do irritating, it seems to me. I am sorry that you have to put up with me. Perhaps my niece Isobel will not enjoy my company for a whole week, if that is the way I am.'

Deirdre Fount walked into the back kitchen, her head held high. But when she returned with the tray of tea, Mrs Oddicott could not let the matter rest. She had been wanting to speak her mind to her daughter for some days, for it had to do with their business, their livelihood, and so she felt that she had a duty.

'Of course,' she said, therefore, taking her cup of tea over to the far side of the shop, 'it would be easier, *much* easier, for me to leave well alone. I would have thought that perhaps you might notice that something was amiss, but you have not noticed, I can no longer rely on you these days.'

'What is amiss?'

'You have just remarked yourself about the emptiness of the shop.'

'Yes.'

'And have you not noticed how empty it has been for some days. For over a week – perhaps even longer.'

'Well, it is the slack time of year. We are building up to the Christmas season.'

'The Christmas season is well under way in all the other shops, as you must have noticed. But do you expect that, within the next week, the shop will be bursting with customers and our takings will reach a record level?'

'We always do very nicely over Christmas, but we are not, after all, a *gift* shop. All the same, there are plenty of interesting buys, we have a good stock. The people will soon begin to arrive.'

'It has nothing to do with the stock.'

'What are you trying to say, mother?'

'Do you think that it *pleases* me to say it, Deirdre . . .'

'It has something to do with me, you think? Is that what you are trying to tell me? People do not come into the shop because of something I have done?'

'You have said it yourself. Though it is not so much a question of anything *done*.'

'Something I have said, then? What have I said? Who has been complaining to you? I am never impolite, I have very great patience with customers, and they can be most difficult, as you know.'

Mrs Oddicott held her cup a little way out and cocked her head slightly on one side.

'Is it not just your whole *attitude*, your whole way of behaving, that has been noticed? I am sure *I* have noticed. You are abstracted and careless and vague, you try to hurry people over their purchases and seem to have no time to listen to their little bits of chatter, you do not offer to put yourself out, if it does not suit you. People like consistency in a shop-keeper, that is a lesson I have had to learn. One cannot let one's own little moods appear on the surface. I am sure there have been many times when I have had a headache, or been a little tired, when my back has been playing me up, and I could so easily have been a little snappy or impatient. But it is all a question of self-control. *I* do not give way, and perhaps you could learn from me, for I do have some years of experience behind me, I am your mother and not perhaps altogether without influence. Or *was* not.

'Well, I will say no more, I will leave you to think about it all. But your mind has been on other things, you have been suffering from some very peculiar moods and the customers have noticed, they are keeping away. I would not be at all surprised to hear that the drapery counter of Hoskins has increased its trade recently.' She set her cup very carefully down on the tray. 'Not at *all* surprised.'

I cannot stand it, thought Deirdre Fount, I shall have to get away, and I do not care how much you suffer as a result. You are not going to ruin my life altogether, I will not be spoken to like that, I will not have such ludicrous accusations fired at me. I will take James and make a new life somewhere a long way off, for I am not old, and there will be opportunities for me in plenty. *You* will be lonely and old and unhappy, and have only yourself to blame.

'There is no need to look at me like that,' said Mrs Winifred Oddicott, who had her back to her daughter and could not see the expression on her face. 'I know what you are thinking and you need not suppose that I am impervious to such resentment and hostility. You were just the same as a child, after I had had to speak to you.'

'Well,' said Aubrey Fount, 'I know very little about boys, I'm afraid.'

'No.'

'No. But I daresay you'd like to go and have tea. That would be all right for you?'

'Yes,' said James, 'thank you.'

He sat back against the deep leather and felt the heater blowing across his legs. Mr Schwartz's Rover had been a big car, too, and smart and comfortable, but different to this, more subdued and perhaps a bit dull. This one had bright red upholstery and a row of switches on the dashboard lit from inside with green and blue lights, and music coming from the radio.

'How about getting away from Westbourne, having a bit of a trip?'

'Yes,' said James, 'thank you.'

Aubrey Fount felt depressed. What a pale boy he is, pale and quiet, he thought, doesn't look to have much about him, doesn't say anything. When the school bell had gone and they had all started to come out, he had tried to pick out the right one and hoped it would be this one, or this, or especially *this*, and all the boys he had picked were tall and strong-looking, they had fought and leaped about and trailed their blazers on the ground. None of them had come up to the car. And then he had seen James and known at once. He was standing very still, belted tightly into an over-large gabardine. His cap was very straight. There had been no point in hoping for anything better, for he had been protected and coddled all through his childhood, he spent all his time with women. Mrs Oddicott would want him clean and neat and silent.

'Is this your own car?' he said now, because it seemed rude

just to sit and look out of the window at the scenery. His mother had told him to talk.

'No, no. Company car, firm's demo model, you see.'

'Oh.'

'I deal in cars, have the pick of the bunch.'

'Oh.'

They accelerated out on to the coast road.

'Like your school, do you, James? Everything all right there?'

'Yes thanks.'

'I suppose you're getting on well at lessons, all that sort of thing?'

'All right, thanks.'

'What games do you play?'

'Soccer. And cricket in summer.'

'I daresay you're in one of the teams, are you . . .'

'No.'

No, thought Aubrey Fount, you are thin and pale and clean and studious-looking, you would never be in any team. Not that he had been himself.

'Of course,' he said, 'I can't show you this car's paces just here, can't work up a good speed on this road.'

'Oh.'

'But enough to give you the feel of the thing.'

'Yes.'

'Feeling all right, are you? Not going to be sick?'

'I'm never sick.'

'Well that's all right, that's a relief,' said Aubrey Fount and then could not think of anything else.

It was a good thing, after all, that he was returning to Birmingham in only a week's time, because his holiday in Westbourne had been a mistake, he should have known that from the beginning. He was bored and depressed, the good intentions about doing his duty as a father had not stood him in any sort of stead. I had better have kept right out of it, he thought now, left well alone, stayed at home and forgotten all about the boy, except for Christmas and birthdays. It is far too late for us to get to know one another, for me to have any influence over him.

The sight of Deirdre had depressed him, too, he did not like to be reminded that once he had chosen to marry her. She had let herself go, you might have expected that. She wore grey and beige and dun-coloured clothes against her pale skin, she was nervous and sexless and he disliked the way her huge, anxious eyes peered into his face.

There had been the girl Yvonne, too, and he ought to have known better than that, he could have chosen much more carefully. Aubrey Fount fiddled with the knob of the radio, flicking through the stations. Yvonne was thirty-two years old and emotional, she had begun to make hysterical statements, that evening in the back of his car, had talked about Involvement and Commitment and Love and the Future.

'I'm learning to play the flute,' said James.

'Oh.'

'In March I shall take the Grade Six exam.'

'Oh? Oh, well I suppose that's very good. Yes, that's a good hobby to have.'

'Can you play an instrument?'

'No. No, I can't say that I can, I'm afraid. Never been much of a one for music, really.'

'Oh.'

They were silent again and Aubrey Fount realized vaguely that they might have talked, if he had been a different sort of person and the boy had been a different boy, but that as it was, they would eat their tea and be embarrassed, and go home with relief. They turned into the drive of the Country Club.

'Tea,' he said loudly, and rubbed his hands together. 'Tea. I daresay you're ready for it?'

'Yes,' said James Fount. 'Thanks.'

He opened the door of the six-seater American saloon and thought that if it were only a question of warm, fast journeys, with the soft upholstery and the radio playing and always tea at the end of them, then he would not mind his father's company.

'Of course,' said Mrs Auriole Carpenter, taking a hand-made chocolate from the box in the glove compartment, 'your father is an old man, we should remember that.'

'He is seventy-three. Not old these days, with all the wonders of modern medicine.'

'But it is time to be realistic. *We* should be thinking of the future and of what arrangements have been made, even if they do not.'

Edward Carpenter drove the maroon Jaguar off the motorway into the service area, for petrol.

'Arrangements?' he said. 'What do you mean, "arrangements"?'

But the pump attendant was ready and waiting.

'I will get out and stretch my legs,' said Auriole Carpenter. But the air was very cold indeed when she opened the car door, and perhaps the sharp blue sky and pale sunshine were best enjoyed from behind the windows, after all.

'I thought you would be wanting some coffee,' said her husband, as she sat down again carefully so as not to crease the pale-blue knitted coat.

'They do not serve anything worth drinking in these places, surely you know that? It is all powdered coffee got up in silver pots.'

Edward Carpenter sighed and reached for a chocolate to console himself.

'I am sure *that* is not a good idea! You ought not to be eating rich chocolates.'

'You have just eaten a rich chocolate.'

'That is a different matter, I am younger and slimmer. And a woman.'

'And why are women entitled to spoil themselves? Am I old and fat?'

'You are going through the coronary years, Edward, how often should I remind you? You need to take plenty of exercise and only plain food. I do try to see to it. You would just eat and drink yourself to death, if it were not for me.'

'Yes,' said Edward Carpenter, and the maroon Jaguar started forward.

'What arrangements?' he asked again, ten miles further on.

Mrs Auriole Carpenter sighed. 'If you must have it spelled out to you, I was thinking about the will. Now do not pretend that you have forgotten all that fuss the Ivies suffered, when Gerald died intestate. It was a great anxiety and trouble. There is no need to go red in the face, no need to look at me like that, I am not one of those monsters who expect everything to be left to them, I am not thinking at all of *who* shall get what, only of practical, business matters. I want you to be saved a lot of fuss and inconvenience, you and your mother.'

'Who is to say that mother will not die first? Or that *I* may not die, since you remind me so regularly of threatened thrombosis. I do not understand why you feel it necessary to talk of this subject all of a sudden.'

'Reading behind the lines of your mother's letter, I would have thought it is plain that your father is in a poor way.'

'No, no, you are exaggerating. Mother did not say that he is *ill*, only that he has suffered a shock since the death of this friend. His own health is not in jeopardy.'

'It is as well to be prepared. I am only thinking of sparing you, Edward, because people so often try to hide from these things, they will never take the clear-headed, common-sense attitude. But you would not thank me if your father were to die and leave all his affairs in disarray. Besides, we have our boys to think of.'

'I am sure you need have no worries on that score, they will be provided for. My father is an honourable man.'

Edward Carpenter spoke very stiffly, and his wife knew when, for the time being at least, to let a matter drop. Instead of talking, she thought about it herself.

No other person was entitled to inherit the Carpenter money, not unless the old man had gone off and made some strange friendship in his recent years. But if it had not been for this talk of his confusion and forgetfulness she would not have worried. Now, anything might happen, he might lose his faculties and linger on and no business could be done, a will might be made on the spur of the moment, leaving out Edward and his family, and then the old man might die and it would be too late. Such things had been known to happen. Our interests ought to be fully protected, thought Mrs Auriole Carpenter, it is Edward's duty to see to it, because there are grandsons to be considered. He shall bring up the matter while we are at the hotel.

'And another thing,' she said aloud.

'What is that?'

'We must get out somewhere on our own during this weekend.'

'Where?'

'It does not in the least matter *where* – anywhere at all, so long as we do not have to spend the whole time cooped up in the hotel with your parents. I hope they will not expect it.'

'But it is to see them that we are travelling all this way. We can scarcely go gallivanting off here, there and everywhere, the moment we arrive.'

'Nobody suggested it, Edward, sometimes I think you do not even listen to what I say. Just an afternoon or evening, that is all I ask, so as to get away and enjoy ourselves. We do not spend very much time together these days.'

Edward Carpenter wondered if this could possibly be true.

'Yes,' he said, as he moved the maroon Jaguar into the fast lane. 'Yes, very well.'

'I did wonder if I might find you here,' said the man called Clifford, from the Borough Engineer's Department.

Yvonne pulled her coat more closely about her and tried to look severe. She was waiting, with a glass of tomato juice, for Aubrey Fount. *You* had your chance, she wanted to say to Clifford, you would have done, but now I know better, now you will not do.

'How are you,' he asked her, 'these days?'

'Oh, fine thank you, *very* well. I am waiting for a friend.'

'Oh yes?'

'At any moment.'

'Ah. Ah, well. Perhaps I can get you something – another glass of that, while you wait?'

'No, thank you.'

'No.'

The door of the Ship and Castle opened, and Yvonne looked up sharply but it was not Aubrey Fount who came in.

'He is just a few minutes late,' she said, 'my friend. So he will be here at any moment now.'

'Good, good. Well – still working in the same office, are you, Yvonne?'

'The same one.'

'Up there on corridor four?'

'Yes.'

He jingled the coins up and down in his trouser pockets. Underneath the sports jacket, he wore a moss-green knitted cardigan, zipped and not buttoned up the front. How *could* I, thought Yvonne, however could I have hoped ... There is nothing to him, just nothing at all.

'I expect you are meeting someone, too,' she said, desperate for him to be gone before Aubrey arrived, for she could never bring herself to introduce them, they would have nothing to say to one another. Besides, Clifford should not think that he had any reason to be introduced to her friends, he should not be allowed to peer and pry into the corners of her private life.

'Won't they be waiting?'

'No, no,' he said. 'No one in particular,' and he shifted from foot to foot, and ran his hand again over the tufts of hair, for the truth was that he did not like to leave her sitting there alone, it looked so bad, on a busy night. He felt sorry for her, that she should be waiting.

'Still, I suppose I had better be getting along, Yvonne. Yes. I had thought of looking in at the Social Club, have a game of snooker perhaps.'

'Yes?'

'Perhaps see you up there sometimes, then?'

'Oh, I very much doubt it.'

'Well – up on corridor four.'

She smiled at him, but rather coldly, and Clifford from the Borough Engineer's Department gave up and went off to finish his beer before leaving the pub, so that she would not have to catch his eye again. Yvonne picked up an evening paper left by someone on the table, and held it up before her face. It was twenty-five minutes past eight, a Friday night. She began to feel conspicuous.

Until the moment after he had watched his son leave the car, walk up the path of the house and shut the door, Aubrey Fount had intended, really *had* intended, to go to the Ship and Castle. It was a quarter to seven, he would eat an early dinner and then meet Yvonne for the last time, and if she tried to prise an address out of him, he would appeal to her trust and discretion, without giving it to her.

But being with James had depressed him, the town of Westbourne depressed him, and the thought of a further week, and the eager Yvonne, depressed him beyond words. Until he thought, well then, I need not meet her, I need not stay in this place another moment, if I do not choose, I can invent some excuse at the hotel, and be on my way tonight.

He cheered up at once, felt almost gay and generous, was nearly tempted to write her a short note. Except that it would never do, never do.

'Something very urgent has cropped up which makes it necessary for me to leave tonight,' he told the desk clerk. 'I shall not be able to stay for a further week. I apologize for the inconvenience, but if you would have my bill ready by the time I come down with my case . . .?'

'I shall have to have a word with the Manager, sir, it may be necessary to charge you for the second week. This is not really . . .'

'No, you will charge me for tonight and have no difficulty in letting the room tomorrow. I will speak to the Manager myself, if it is not arranged.'

Aubrey Fount walked masterfully towards the lift. That is the way to behave in public places, he thought, that is the way to talk. There is no need to grovel, no need to let them talk of this and that hotel rule, simply pay what is owed for one week, and walk out.

At ten minutes to nine, Yvonne, who was embarrassed by the glances from people in the bar, asked for the use of the public telephone. He is ill, she thought, he has had an accident, is lying somewhere, injured and alone. I have been sitting here waiting selfishly, when he is in some trouble.

'Mr Fount, Madam? Just one moment.'

The telephone booth smelled of 'Arpège'.

'I'm sorry, Madam, Mr Fount checked out of the hotel half an hour ago.'

'No, no, there must be some mistake. Perhaps there is another guest of that name. He cannot have left.'

'I'm sorry, Madam.'

'Please check again.'

'Very well.'

But the girl with the impersonal voice only came back after a moment, and said that Mr Fount had undoubtedly gone.

'Gone? Gone altogether? Are his bags packed, is his bill paid? He *cannot* have gone.'

'He has gone, Madam, half an hour or more ago.'

Then he will be here soon, thought Yvonne, he must be planning to see me and then drive back home later. Or perhaps he will take me with him, *that* may be the plan.

She returned to the lounge bar. Her seat there was taken and no other was vacant.

'All alone, darling? Have a drink with me?'

Yvonne walked quickly out of the Ship and Castle and caught a bus along the Esplanade to the Prince of Wales Hotel. But yes, yes, Mr Fount had certainly gone, change of plan, he had said, tonight and not at the end of next week. No, no, of course no address, even if they would pass it on. No, and no message either.

'His car?' Yvonne said. 'What about his car? If that is still in the garage he cannot have gone.'

'I will check with the garage, Madam. One moment.'

But the car had gone, half an hour ago, the garage said. Yvonne clenched her fists deep inside her coat pockets, and left the hotel.

On the coast road, Aubrey Fount picked up two girls who were hitch-hiking, and the red-headed one sat right up to him in the front seat of the American saloon. He did not think again about Yvonne, though he did wonder if it would be a good idea to let Miriam know he was back.

'He is growing up to be secretive,' said Mrs Winifred Oddicott. 'Just like you.'

'I daresay he is tired.'

Deirdre Fount began to tack carefully around the edges of the paper pattern.

'Or sick.'

'Why ever should he be sick, mother?'

'In that great car, on top of a huge tea.'

'So you *did* look out of the window! You did see the car.'

'Yes, I did and I must say I thought it typical, only what we would have expected from Aubrey Fount. So flashy and taking up half the road. They will have driven all over the countryside at a hundred miles an hour, for that is the only way he would know of trying to impress the boy, and James will be feeling sick – perhaps he has already been sick. Have you asked him if he has been sick?'

'Of course I have not. He is a grown boy.'

'I do not like to think what tales he has been hearing, or what nonsense Aubrey has filled his ears with.'

'Oh, I *knew* there was something I had forgotten to tell you, mother,' Deirdre Fount looked up enthusiastically from her dressmaking, anxious to change the subject. 'I read it in the paper. There has been a report that Frankie Vaughan may be appearing in the pantomime at Edinburgh this year. Now fancy that! You cannot deny that you have a very soft spot for him, you are always saying he is one of the few real singers left. Of course it has not been settled, they only said, "negotiations are under way," which means it might all be cancelled. But wouldn't it be splendid?'

'Would it? In what way splendid? What has that to do with me?'

'Why, because you will be in Edinburgh right after Christmas, you will be able to go and see their pantomime.'

'Will I? Do not be too sure of that.'

'But they would be so pleased to take you. Or you might take *them*. Yes, you could take the children. I daresay they are just the right age to enjoy a good pantomime.'

'I meant, Deirdre, that I may not be in Edinburgh at all.'

'Of course you will be there, we have discussed it and it is all settled.'

'*You* may have everything settled, *your* holiday may be all arranged, but please do not try and run my life for me, I am not yet in my dotage. I can decide what I want to do for myself.'

'But you have written to Isobel and she has said what a good idea it is, she is going to be looking forward to your visit. You cannot suddenly change your mind.'

'I hope it is still my privilege.'

'Very well. But *why*? You need a holiday as much as I do and you will enjoy yourself in Edinburgh, it will make a complete change.'

'That is what you tell me, and tell yourself, that is what you have been saying so often, in order to salve your own conscience. To justify your selfishness you say that *I* need a holiday, and now you try and butter me up with talk of singers and pantomimes. Well, I may be an old woman in your eyes, Deirdre, but I am not entirely stupid, not blind, and your cunning has always been so transparent! Ever since you were a very small girl, you have thought to sneak behind my back to get your own way, and you never gave me credit for being your own mother, for spotting what you were trying to do almost before you did it, you were obsessed by what you thought was your own cleverness. Well, let me tell you that I may not go to Edinburgh because I may wish to stay here and keep the shop open. I am not at all convinced of the sense in closing for a full week; we may lose much of the goodwill we have built up in this town.'

'What nonsense!'

'Do not forget that it is *my* shop, Deirdre, it is in my name, and if I choose to stay open and manage alone, that is my affair.'

'You are saying this to make me feel guilty, to make me change my mind and stay at home. That is all.'

'Oh, no!'

'Yes. But you need not, because I warn you, mother, that I shall not succumb to your moral blackmail, I have had quite enough.' And Deirdre Fount began to cut vigorously through the cloth with her sharp, dressmaker's scissors.

'Or,' said Mrs Winifred Oddicott sweetly, 'I may go elsewhere, I may take a short holiday by myself.'

'That is up to you.'

'I am glad you admit it. I will not be pushed from pillar to post by my own daughter.'

'Very well.'

'I do not have to consult you about any of my affairs.'

'I was trying to think of you, trying to arrange something you would enjoy, but you must do as you think fit.' She laid down her scissors. 'I am going upstairs to have a word with James.'

'And if you have any sense of responsibility you will tell him how impolite he is, to come straight in and go up to his room with barely a word of greeting, and such a sullen face, without a thought that anyone might need his help or want his company. You are his mother, and he must learn these things from you.'

But Deirdre Fount did not say anything about it. She sat on the edge of the bed and picked at a flaw in the welt of her son's discarded pullover, and thought, I am afraid of him. For he was a silent, quite unpredictable boy.

'Is that homework, dear?' For she did not want to begin by talking about his father.

'Sort of.'

'Oh? I think it either is or it isn't, don't you?'

'It's a project.'

'I see. And who is it for?'

'Mr Sargent.'

'That's biology, isn't it?'

'Geography.'

'I remember!'

James Fount breathed very carefully over the tracing of a map.

'And where did you go for tea?'

'I don't know – in the country. A big sort of place, like a hotel.'

'I can't think where that might have been.'

'A club.'

'A . . . Oh, the *Country* Club? Well, that must have been very nice. What sort of things did you eat?'

'Egg on toast. And cakes. You know.'

There was silence. Make it easier, thought Deirdre Fount, why can you not help me to talk to you? Other boys talk, their mothers do not sit and feel as though they were in the company of strangers. For she looked across at James, as she sat on the striped quilt of his bed, and saw that there was no one else, now that she had broken with her mother, and Aubrey was gone again. I will make a new life soon, she told herself, new friends. I will have my hair well cut and permed, I will colour in the grey bits and make myself two smart outfits with toning accessories, I will pluck the hairs from between my eyebrows and read, to inform myself about interesting topics, and when I have done that, I will make my plans, I will step out boldly, I will meet people and they will talk to me in a friendly way. Perhaps I may marry again, for I am not quite forty, when all is said and done, I am not going to give in now, this is not the end.

But for the moment there was only James.

'Your father would have been pleased to see you,' she said.

'Oh.'

'Well of course he would!'

'He hasn't been before, has he?'

'No, No, but – well, it is not always easy, things are not quite so straightforward as they may seem to you, dear, you cannot altogether understand the circumstances.'

'I liked his car.'

'Did you?'

'He must be rich. Pretty rich.'

'I know it isn't ideal,' Deirdre Fount said hurriedly, staring at the yellow-painted wardrobe, 'living with your grandmother. Of course there is school and so on for you, but I do see that it must make things rather hard.'

'What things?'

'Well – not having a father always at home.'

'Prentice hasn't got a father. He got killed. He went out on the lifeboat.'

'Oh dear!'

'It's all right, he was only a baby. He doesn't remember him.'

'No, but he will understand, not having a father at home, either. He will have the same problems as you. Is Prentice your friend?'

'Not really.'

'Oh. I don't want you to feel that you are missing things, dear, the sort of life other boys have.'

James Fount went on inking the northern sections of his map.

'That's why we are going on holiday.'

'Are we? When are we?'

'For the week after Christmas. A very special sort of holiday.'

'Abroad? Are we going on a ski-ing holiday? That's what the Fellows do, they go every year. This year they're going to Davos.'

'Oh!'

'Are we?'

'No, dear. I am sorry, but I don't think we could manage that – I couldn't afford it.'

Though I know that we could, thought Deirdre Fount, it is only that I am too nervous, I would not know how to go about it and it has been hard enough to tell my mother of these arrangements. I would not know how to get along with the people there, and James is very young to go abroad.

'I really meant that it will be a special sort of holiday because it will be just you and I. We are going to a lovely comfortable hotel in the country.'

'What sort of country? Wild country?'

'Well ...'

'Is it mountains? Is it the Trossachs?' Because he was just then lettering them on his map.

'Goodness me, no! That is in Scotland, dear, and it would be very bleak and cold in winter.'

'Like Switzerland.'

'We are going to the Cotswolds. To Gloucestershire.'

'Oh. What to do?'

'If you ask your Mr Sargent, perhaps he will tell you about the countryside there. It is so beautiful, and this little hotel is in one of the old towns and overlooks a bit of the river, with woods all behind. We can go for walks. But of course we might go into Cheltenham and Cirencester, places like that, and make some of the excursions to the Cathedrals round about. All that sort of thing.'

'Is that all?'

'It will be a lovely rest for me, you see, James, away from the shop and so on.'

'Oh.'

'We don't spend very much time together, do we, just the two of us? It will be a chance for us to get to know one another.'

Downstairs the telephone rang, and went on ringing, because Mrs Winifred Oddicott refused to answer it.

When his mother had gone, James Fount looked out of the window at the dark back garden and wondered however he might get out of going on the awful holiday.

Chapter Nine

'HIS face,' said Major Bertram Carpenter, helping himself to sauté potatoes, 'went the colour of a bad egg. Just those last few moments. The colour of a bad egg.'

Across the table his daughter-in-law looked pained. He had been talking about the death of Mr Isepp for some time.

Mrs Auriole Carpenter wore a model dress of oyster-grey silk grosgrain, to accompany which she had forced her husband to wear a dinner jacket.

'It is a four-star hotel,' she had said, 'and it is Saturday night. That is why I put the jacket in your overnight case. It is only correct.'

'Nobody else will be wearing them, people do not, these days.'

'Then we shall set them an example. I will never have it said that *my* standards are dropping and that I do not know the correct procedures and how things ought to be. Besides, you should enjoy looking your best, Edward, you should enjoy wearing good clothes as much as you enjoy eating good food and drinking good wine.'

'My father will not be wearing one.'

'Oh, I am sure he will not, I do not remember the last time I saw your father wear anything but that mould-green sports jacket. What your father does or does not is surely no criterion, Edward.'

'I would not wish to embarrass him.'

But Mrs Auriole Carpenter had only met his eye in the mirror and said nothing more, so that now, he sat beside her wearing the dinner jacket.

'It shook me,' said Major Bertram Carpenter, 'taught me a thing or two about the ways of these doctors and their hospitals, I can tell you.'

'Have a little more potato,' said his wife, for she had noticed the expression on her daughter-in-law's face.

'I would not,' said Major Carpenter, 'you please yourself, but I do not recommend their potatoes.'

'You have a large helping on your plate at the moment, father.'

'Yes, and you have never complained about it before, Bertram. What is wrong? I always think they do their potatoes especially well here, they are so nice and crisp.'

'They are indigestible.'

'Oh, surely not!'

'*You* would not know anything about it, Flora, you have a constitution of cast-iron, nothing affects you and you are always asleep the moment your head touches the pillow. But I may say that I have suffered badly these past few nights, and even during the day, too. I have been in considerable discomfort solely on account of their potato.'

'Then you had better not eat it,' said Mrs Auriole Carpenter, a trifle sharply, 'it is as simple as that. You see, Edward, *there* are some people in evening dress, did I not tell you? How very much better they look, how very suitable and smart in a hotel of this kind.'

'Perhaps they are going to a theatre.'

'There is no theatre for forty miles.'

'Or a concert.'

'Edward, don't be facetious.'

Major Bertram Carpenter snorted and thought how much fatter his son had become, and how little of interest he had to say for himself. And indeed, Edward Carpenter sat and thought of nothing at all, only ate his way through the duckling and felt stiff and conspicuous in his dinner jacket.

Mrs Auriole Carpenter surveyed the long dining room and priced the guests and thought that tomorrow they must get out, spend a long morning in some comfortable place drinking cocktails, or else she would go quite mad with the boredom of it all.

Whichever one of them dies first, she thought – and smiled at her mother-in-law across the table – I could never give a permanent home to the other, I could not put up with either of them. It would be unfair to them, too, for I should make them unhappy, we live an entirely different sort of life and none of us could cope, they would be quite out of place. Perhaps they could move a little *nearer* but that is as far as it could go. I must mention it to Edward, for he is still quite sure that I am worrying unnecessarily, he has not noticed his father's bad colour, and slightly bloodshot eyes.

'He has gone!' said Mrs Flora Carpenter suddenly, 'that is what I meant to tell you, Bertram, and there is something else even more interesting about it.'

'Who? Who has gone where? You expect me to follow your silent trains of thought and take up with whatever remark you throw out, but it cannot be done, Flora, you must make yourself clear. *Who* has gone?'

'The man with the red moustache. Surely you remember?'

'The salesman.'

'We did not *know* that, Bertram, you really should not . . .'

'Never mind, go on, go on. What about this man? You have been remarkably interested in him all along, and I am sure I cannot see why. Common-looking fellow, I thought, with a shifty expression. He had nothing to do with us.'

'His name was *Fount*!' said Mrs Carpenter, 'Mr Fount! There, does that not interest and intrigue you?'

'Fount? What is so strange or remarkable about the name of Fount? It is a common name, I daresay.'

'No, no, of course it is not. You do not hear of Fount as you hear of Smith and Jones, or even of Carpenter.'

'You have a very poor memory, Flora, that is all I can say. We know a woman by the name of Fount, in this very town, I told you that she was in here the other night talking of Isepp, and do not tell me you have forgotten about *that*. So there is another Fount that I have thought of straight away. I will have the cheese,' he said to the waiter. 'Plain cheddar cheese, if you please. Your puddings give me indigestion.'

'Do you not see, Bertram, that if we know a Mrs Fount in this town – and she is not a widow, you know, there is a divorced husband somewhere – and if a *Mr* Fount arrived to stay alone for a week at a hotel in the same town . . .'

'Rum baba,' said Edward Carpenter, pointing to the trolley.

'Dear Edward, are you *sure* that is a good idea? They are very rich and after the duck, too, you will . . .'

'Perfectly right,' said Major Bertram Carpenter, unexpectedly, 'your wife is perfectly right for once, Edward, you are grossly overweight, and if you over-eat you will soon have a heart attack. Men do.'

'Oh, father, I am so relieved to hear you add your voice to mine on that subject. I tell him and tell him about it and I do not think he takes the least notice. I am very concerned. He *is* overweight, he must be careful.'

The waiter stood by, smiling a little.

'I will have rum baba,' said Edward Carpenter, and then stared defiantly down at his napkin.

'Yes, yes dear,' said his mother, 'of course you shall, for this is a holiday, you know, we are all here to enjoy ourselves and so we shall have just what we want, be self-indulgent for once in a way.'

'I am eating cheese, plain cheddar cheese.'

'Profiteroles,' said Mrs Flora Carpenter, and her eyes lit up. 'Profiteroles and cream! Yes, how delicious!'

'There is a Lord Chief Justice Fount,' said Mrs Auriole Carpenter, 'or so I believe. Perhaps this was the man.'

'Nonsense, he was a salesman, no question about it, and nobody has yet explained to me what all this fuss about a strange hotel guest called Fount has to do with us. It is all so much gibberish, I am quite in the dark.'

'I am suggesting that he was the divorced husband of Mrs Deirdre Fount, Bertram, that is all. It seems more than likely, especially in view of her having visited the hotel that night. Mrs Fount keeps the little drapery shop, Auriole, with her mother Mrs Oddicott. A nice girl, really, so I can only think that the blame of the divorce is not hers. But he was such a pleasant man, he spoke to me in the Red Lounge one afternoon over tea, and he had what you would call a *cultured* voice, I confess I had not expected it.'

'You will hobnob with anyone,' said Major Carpenter, through a mouthful of cream cracker, 'in the lounges over tea.'

'I am quite fascinated to think that there may be a reunion, you know.'

In a few moments, thought Mrs Auriole Carpenter, I shall scream, I shall tell them loudly that if they have nothing of more interest than this to talk about, they would do better to be silent, for I confess I cannot stand it. I have so little patience because we are used to such a high level of conversation with our own friends at home. How appalling to be old and to be so entirely taken up with trivialities, to be failing and have such narrow horizons. How pitiable to demand company and sympathy, and receive them only because you are old.

Edward Carpenter and his father began to talk spiritedly about the fate of the Argyll and Sutherland Highlanders.

How nice, thought Mrs Flora Carpenter, how very nice to see them like this, how splendid that they have not really grown apart, that an old man and his son can still get on.

Oh, it is all very well, thought her daughter-in-law, it is all very well for *men*!

When it happened it was like a miracle. It could not really be an answer to prayer, because James Fount had not thought to pray, he had only turned the subject over and over in his mind and wished and wished until he saw the hopelessness of wishing, and began to despair. In a week's time they would break up for Christmas and in two weeks' time he would go with his mother to the Cotswold hotel and there was nothing anybody could do about it.

And then it had happened.

'Wait for me,' Schwartz had said in the corridor, 'wait for me downstairs.'

'Schwartz, you are talking.'

'Yes, sir.'

'You know perfectly well that you do not talk to and from assembly.'

'Yes, sir.'

'You will go and see the Headmaster at four o'clock. I have had enough of you this week, Schwartz.'

'Please, sir, I am already going to see him.'

'Then you should be ashamed of yourself.'

'Yes, sir.'

But he had managed to get out, 'I've got to ask you something,' on his way through the hall doors.

James Fount waited outside the cloakroom huts in the rain,

belted and buttoned into his long gabardine mac. A week ago he had thought that something might soon come to change his life. A week ago his father was due to arrive and anything might happen. But his father had come and been a disappointment and gone again at once. Nothing at all had happened.

Schwartz came out of the cloakroom.

'What did he do? You weren't so long.'

'Oh, talked, you know. The usual.'

'Oh.'

'And some reading to do and go and see him about. Nothing much.'

James Fount admired Schwartz, and envied him. He himself did not attract attention and trouble, although he was not especially well-behaved.

'What have you got to tell me, anyway?'

'The week after Christmas we're going to Scotland. My father and brother and me. On a railway holiday.'

'What's that?'

'Looking at railways, of course, what do you think? And going on as many as we can and looking at engine sheds and so on. Scotland's good for railways.'

'Great!'

'We might take a caravan unless the weather's awful. I expect it will be, so we'll stay in a hotel and go off for days. But the caravan's best.'

'What about cooking?'

'My father cooks of course. He's a very good cook.'

'Oh.'

'And I can do beans and things. Well, anyone can do beans, can't they?'

'I don't know.'

James Fount would never have admitted to the confident and worldly Schwartz that he was not allowed to touch the cooker, had never cracked open an egg or fried bacon or done more than tip the kettle on to the tea-leaves or turned out cornflakes into a bowl.

'I do not like the idea of men in kitchens, I will not have a grandson who is treated like a girl,' Mrs Winifred Oddicott always said.

'Want to come with us?' asked Schwartz.

They were pushing their feet through the last mouldering leaves. James Fount stopped.

'You can. My father said to ask you, he said I could bring anyone I wanted and I said you and that was all right. They like you.'

'Oh.'

'Well then?'

'I'll have to ask. My mother is supposed to be taking me away.'

'Where to?'

'Somewhere in the country.'

'Will you see your father again?'

'Oh, no. Just on a holiday, in a hotel.'

'What will you do?'

'I don't know. Nothing much. It's so that my mother can have a rest, I think.'

'Oh. Oh well, you don't have to go then, do you? You could easily come with us.'

'I'm not sure.'

'Well, you'd *rather*, wouldn't you? It'll be great and who wants to go with their mother to a mouldy hotel in the country?'

'She might say no.'

'You can make her change her mind, can't you? They generally say no to start with until you go on and on about it, and make them think. I can make my parents do anything I want.'

'Oh.'

'All right then, if you don't want to come with us.'

'Don't be stupid, I'd much rather, I don't want to go with her at all.'

'Ask her then?'

'Yes.'

'Now? Come on, I'll go with you if you like, and wait, and then I can tell her all about it so she'll know it's O.K.'

'She won't be there now.'

'All right, we'll go to the shop.'

'No, I don't think so.'

'Why not?'

'Well . . . O.K. then. Yes, come on, we'll go to the shop and I'll ask her. She's got to say yes, she's got to let me.

'Race you.'

Schwartz and Fount began to run.

Mark Schwartz picked up a cardboard box full of pins and balanced it delicately on end, at the very edge of the counter.

'It's rotten,' said James Fount, 'I don't see what's wrong with it, I don't see why I can't go. I think it's rotten, I think *you're* rotten.'

Mrs Winifred Oddicott glanced at her daughter, at the set, hurt expression and the wide-open, protruding eyes, and smiled. But I will not say anything, she thought, it is not for me to say that I could see this, or something like this, coming, and that she has only herself to blame. I will not say, *Now* perhaps you understand, now you know what it feels like to be treated with insolence and contempt by your own child. The true character of that boy is rapidly showing itself and I am very sorry to see it, he has been spoiled beyond repair and I am ashamed, though perhaps not very surprised.

But I will take no part in this argument, I will stand here and be silent. Though why the boy should not go on a holiday with his friend, especially a family like that of Mark Schwartz, the sort of people we ought to be delighted to get to know, *I* am sure I cannot think. This whole scheme of Deirdre's for a week in the country while I am pushed off to Scotland is foolish and selfish, and who can blame the boy for wanting to go elsewhere? I am sure I cannot.

Aloud, she only said, 'I suppose we ought to be thankful that there are no customers in the shop. I would not like anyone to witness a family scene on business premises.'

Deirdre Fount ignored her, and went on staring over the counter at her son.

'I think you ought to say yes, anyway, you've *got* to say yes. It'll be the best holiday I've ever had, nobody will ever ask me on another holiday like it, not ever again. It isn't fair.'

'Oh, how unkind and thoughtless, James! I am surprised at you. It is only yesterday that I told you about my plans for *our* holiday, and you seemed so pleased.'

Though Deirdre Fount knew that he had not, he had said nothing, only worked away at the drawing of his map.

'You ought to be very grateful, for it is not everyone who has the chance to stay in a lovely comfortable hotel, with a room all to himself. I am only trying to please you, and there would be so many interesting things to do.'

'No, there wouldn't, there wouldn't be anything, not anything at all. It's *your* holiday, not my holiday. Who wants to go to a rotten hotel in the Cotswolds? *I* don't, I want to go with Schwartz.'

James Fount wished that he might scream and beat his fists on the counter to make her understand his anger and frustration, and the unfairness of it all, for it had seemed to be like a miracle and now she would not let the miracle take place. But he could do nothing, he spoke in a low, tight voice and spun the revolving button display round and round with his hand, while Schwartz played with the box of pins and was silent. James Fount could see the expression of pity on his face, and the amazement that any friend of his should have such a parent. But soon Schwartz would give up being sorry and surprised, he would shrug his shoulders and begin to mock and despise and then he would ask someone else to go on the railway holiday, and James Fount would no longer be his friend.

'Oh, I *must* go,' he said, and his skin felt prickly and hot, and he wanted to scratch and scratch at it with his nails. 'You have to let me go.'

Deirdre Fount looked at her son and thought more than ever before that he had nothing to do with her, she did not know him, for she had never before seen him like this, white with rage and frustration. He clenched his fists as he swung the button stand round and round.

But I will not give in, she thought, I will not pander to him. All my life I have given in to the moral blackmail from my mother, and I will not suffer it now from my eleven-year-old son. James is coming on holiday with me, I deserve a rest and a change, I deserve his company, for I have no one else. Besides, it will be good for him.

'When you get there,' she said, 'you will enjoy yourself. I am very sorry, Mark, and it is most kind of your mother to offer –

I shall write and thank her – but it is out of the question, you see our holiday is already booked and arranged. If it had been another time – well, but it is not and there is an end.'

She opened the till and began to count change, so that she would not have to look any more at her son.

'Oh well,' said Schwartz. 'Come on, then.'

James Fount stood still.

'Maybe we'll ask you another time, and you'll be able to come.'

'No,' said James Fount, 'no, you won't. It's this time, I wanted to go *this* time.'

'Oh, well.'

In desperation, Mrs Deirdre Fount took a ten shilling note out of the till and held it across the counter.

'I know,' she said brightly, 'why do you not take Mark across to the Laurel Leaf Café for tea. You may buy whatever you like, it is my treat and I shall not mind how many ice creams you eat or how many meringues, and you need not bring back any change. There, that will cheer you up, James, and when you have finished, you will see, everything will be better, you will soon start looking forward to *our* holiday.'

James Fount stared at his mother across the glass-topped counter, and she saw the plain truth in his eyes, and shrank back from it. 'No thanks,' he said stiffly, 'I don't want any money,' and he turned and walked out of the shop behind his friend Schwartz. As the door banged, the cardboard box full of pins overbalanced and crashed open upon the floor.

Mrs Winifred Oddicott began to hum.

I have done wrong, thought Deirdre Fount, when she woke in the middle of the night. I have done wrong and it is a judgement upon me. I have quarrelled with my mother and spoken harsh words to her, I have wished her dead, I have made her unhappy and cannot help it. But now my own son will not look me in the eyes, and he will think about me in the same way, and talk about me with his friends. As soon as he is able, he will go away.

She put on her blue woollen dressing-gown, knowing that she would not be able to sleep any more, and sat beside the window looking out. All the houses down the avenue were set back in pairs, curtained and shuttered and dark. I have no friends, thought Deirdre Fount, it is my own fault that I have no friends to call on. But not *only* my fault, surely. Others must be equally to blame.

My son hates me and I have failed in every way where he is concerned, I have tried – nobody could say that I have not tried, I have worked hard for him, wanted to bring him up nicely and make him into a good man. But I have failed. I have antagonized him and he will go away. She remembered his face, and the look in his grey eyes across the glass-topped counter that afternoon. He would rather be with strangers, she thought, and that is what my mother says of me.

But after a short time of sitting in despair and weeping a little on to the woollen sleeve of her sensible dressing-gown, Mrs Fount decided that there was a solution, after all. If I tell him that he may go away with his friend Schwartz, she thought, on this railway holiday of theirs, then all will be well, he will brighten at once, for he is only sulking and trying to use his sulks as a weapon, as children will do. But he will no longer look at me with resentment and hatred, if I tell him that he may go. It is as simple as that.

It seemed to be a good idea, too, that her son should cultivate the friendship of people like the Schwartzes. Except that, if she were to do all this she would have to face the Cotswold holiday alone. She thought of sitting at the smallest table in the dining room, eating rapid, solitary meals and being stared at covertly and speculated upon by other women.

Oh why, why, she thought suddenly, did I not do more about Aubrey, why did I behave in such a weak and embarrassed way when he came to see me? He stayed in a hotel across the town all alone, and I could have taken courage and tried to make a new relationship. It was because I am a coward, and because of my mother, that is why. It was out of the question, nothing could have been done, and besides, he did not seem to want it.

But even an eleven-year-old son would have been company in the Cotswold hotel, and would also have given her some confidence.

Now, she would be like all women alone in all the hotels of

the world, arranging little treats for herself and eating too much cake at tea and fussing about the details of her room, talking to other women in strident tones.

I cannot do it, Deirdre Fount thought, it is so unfair. I am not quite forty years of age; do I have to give in to such a way of life already? For some people, these are the best, the most energetic and zestful years, and why not for me? I would rather change my plans altogether. I could go to a winter sports centre, full of unattached younger people, or to London, where there is always entertainment, always the chance of meeting someone interesting and new.

But it was impossible, she would never pluck up sufficient courage, and there was her mother to be considered. 'A holiday *alone*,' she would say sharply, 'Well that does strike me as a little odd, Deirdre. You plan to go off to some strange place by yourself, while I manage the shop and spend an uncomfortable week in Edinburgh? Not that I am complaining, and not that I am hinting to come with you, oh no. But I am sure you cannot have thought about it, for you will not enjoy yourself at all, there will be nobody to talk to and nobody to make excursions with. You will sit about in the lounge reading the same page of a book over and over again, and looking conspicuous.'

Outside it began to rain.

Why should I allow myself to be so influenced by my mother, thought Deirdre Fount? All my life I have bowed down to her, agreed with her, taken her word for this and that, all my life she has made me afraid of strange people and new situations, she has reined me in and belittled me, sapped all my confidence. Well, I shall make my decision, I have said so before. This *will* be the start of my new life. James shall go with his friend to look at railways and he will be gay and happy, and when he returns we will talk about it together. Perhaps he will introduce me to Mrs Schwartz and she will invite me there to tea, we shall become friends.

I shall go in and tell him now, not wait for tomorrow morning. I shall wake him and he will be full of delight. She wanted to stand at the side of his bed while he slept and look down fondly at him, for as a baby he had rarely woken, even when teething, and there had been few excuses to get up in the night, and go to comfort him. Even now, the moment she opened his door, he cheated her, by waking at once.

'Only me, dear, only me.'

'Oh.'

He watched her carefully, his face blank and closed to expression.

'I had to come and tell you, James, I had to come and say that I have changed my mind. I was so sharp to you earlier on, I really did not think, but I was a little upset, you see, a little worried. Perhaps you can understand that.'

She sat down on the edge of his bed. James Fount said nothing.

'I have been thinking such a lot about it, it has kept me awake, and of course I do see now that there is no question about it, none at all. You must go on the holiday with your friend, if that is what you want. You would enjoy yourself so much better than with me. So I will say yes. There! You may go with Schwartz. Now, is that all right? Is that what you wanted?'

He turned his head away from her, and after a moment or two, closed his eyes.

'Yes,' he said. 'Yes. Thank you very much.'

Nothing else. Nothing at all even when she kissed him and made a show of patting the pillow and smoothing the coverlet, tucking in the edges of the sheets. He lay quite stiff and still, and pretended to be asleep.

He does not love me, thought Deirdre Fount, he is ungrateful after all. It has done no good and now I have burned my bridges, I must go on this holiday alone, or ask my mother to come, and that I will never do. James is like his father, selfish, thinking always of himself. He does not care and I have no one.

James Fount slept.

Chapter Ten

MISS VIOLET PRUG unwrapped her parcel from Harrods. 'Well,' she said to her companion, Mrs Christie, 'we shall spend a very quiet Christmas.' And she patted the little pile of glossy books that the parcel had contained.

Mrs Christie looked at the detective story and the three new novels of Regency Brighton and felt depressed. As a young girl she had been in service at one of the great Scottish castles and when Christmas came there had been a staff ball and presents from the tree, and dances in all the establishments for miles around. They had travelled together in excited, highly-scented groups when their day's work was done, and life had seemed full of camaraderie and promise.

'Oh, I miss it,' she said now to Miss Prug, 'all that glitter and all the dancing, the lovely dresses we had, even though we did make them ourselves out of this and that. We did not miss out on the enjoyment and the gaiety because we were staff, you know, we had our full share. And the snow, of course. We *always* had snow at Christmas in Scotland when I was a girl.'

'Yes,' said Miss Violet Prug. 'Yes, yes.'

'I have always liked a lot of people about me, at Christmas time.'

'You will go home for the New Year,' said Miss Prug, a little surprised, 'I understand that that is the important time in Scotland. You will go to your sister, for that is what we have arranged long ago, that is what you wanted. But if you would rather go now, you have only to say. I would not want you to stay here with me and be miserable.'

'Oh, no!' said Mrs Christie, shocked at the idea that she might want to give up her Hogmanay. 'No, no, I was only remembering, only just thinking aloud.'

Though it was true that if it was to be only the two of them, and if Miss Prug had her new books, so as to avoid any card games, then it would be a little dull, even though they were eating their Christmas dinner and tea at the Prince of Wales Hotel. It would be just a little dull.

The rich Miss Prug laid her hand on the topmost book. But she would not open it, not yet, not before Christmas. It was a little treat, and she would save it. There were, after all, only three days to go.

On the night of Christmas Eve, Major Bertram Carpenter lay awake and felt whatever food had disagreed with him at supper lying heavy on his stomach. I am suffering, he thought, in spite of bottle after bottle of bismuth and magnesia and all manner of other widely advertised preparations. They have made not a scrap of difference. The cooking is going to seed in this hotel, they are using unrefined fats and artificial sweetenings, we have too much starch and it is all making me ill.

'Flora!' he said aloud, suddenly, '*Flora*. Why do you not wake? Flora?'

Mrs Carpenter muttered, and turned.

'I have a bad pain, I am suffering constantly with this indigestion, in spite of all the care I take over my diet.'

Mrs Flora Carpenter sat up and switched on the light.

'Oh dear! Bertram, I am so sorry, and I am worried about you, but you are so difficult, dear. If only you would see a doctor! For I do not really know how I can help you.'

'Do not talk to me of doctors. Have I not made myself sufficiently clear on that subject?'

'Yes, dear. Would you like me to ring for some hot water? That may soothe you.'

'Nothing soothes me.'

'The bismuth . . .'

'I have taken spoon after spoonful of bismuth, I am soaked in bismuth, and it is of no use.'

'I wish there was something else I could give you, dear.'

'Yes. It is all very well for you, sleeping and snoring.'

'I was snoring? I *am* sorry.'

'And tomorrow, to make matters worse, it is Christmas.'

'Worse? Oh, but you should enjoy your Christmas, Bertram!

You know how lovely it always is in the hotel and there are several families this year with children, I have noticed them about the place, getting excited.'

'It is nothing but a pantomime,' said Major Carpenter, 'the older I get the more clearly I see that it is nothing more than an expensive pantomime. But I am thinking just at this moment of the rich and indigestible food I shall be expected to eat during the next few days.'

'My dear, you do not *have* to eat any of it! If you would just stick to plain breast of turkey, with creamed potatoes, and avoid the puddings and pies and so on . . .'

'Yes, yes, I can see that you have no real idea of what I suffer. Advice is easy to give.'

'But . . .'

'It is a poor show if I cannot even enjoy myself during the festive season. You will be telling the chef to serve me bread and milk, next.'

'I am sorry, Bertram dear. I do know how trying it must be to have such pain all the time, but if only you would just see one doctor, it would all be so simple, he would give you something to cure this once and for all. I cannot understand what makes you so stubborn about it.'

'You cannot understand . . .?' Major Carpenter sat up in bed and stared at his wife. 'Did I hear you say that you cannot understand why I am loath to see a doctor? I, who saw . . .'

'Yes, yes, your friend Mr Isepp, I have not forgotten, of course I have not. But that was the hospital, dear. No one is suggesting that you visit the hospital.'

'I should hope not, by God.'

'But Doctor Rogers has nothing whatsoever to do with the hospital, and he was so very good to you last winter, over your bronchitis.'

'They are all the same, they are all in the same league, Flora.'

'No, no. I am sure . . .'

'Well, I do not want to sit up half the night arguing and chattering, if you please. Let us have the light out, let us get whatever sleep we can manage.'

Mrs Flora Carpenter turned off the lamp, and then lay thinking about her husband's persistent indigestion and what it might signify, and of her son and his wife, who had refused an invitation to spend Christmas, with their boys, here at the hotel.

The little bedside clock struck twelve, it *is* Christmas, thought Mrs Flora Carpenter, it is Christmas now, and here I am like a girl, still excited!

In the next bed, Major Carpenter snored.

I do not want it to happen, thought Mrs Deirdre Fount, waking as usual at seven o'clock. I do not want it to be Christmas. For everyone else is going to parties, the magazines have been full of spangled dresses and hair-pieces and recipes for hot punch, everyone else will receive expensive presents and be surrounded by friends and family whom they find it no strain to love. But here, we are to sit and put on bright faces and make little jokes. My mother will sing in the kitchen and wear a funny hat, and we will drink a glass of medium sweet sherry and James will be fidgeting and fidgeting until it is time for him to be off with his friend Schwartz. And then there will be the long evening alone with my mother, who will crack nuts and pick them delicately out from the spaces between her teeth, and only turn on the television after we have played a ritual game of two-handed whist or snakes and ladders, to celebrate its being Christmas.

We will say less and less to one another as the day wears on, for fear of someone speaking out and saying too much. If there were something to look forward to, some guests or an outing, things might be endured, but there is only my holiday alone, and her holiday – for Mrs Oddicott had decided at the last minute, to go to the niece in Edinburgh.

I do not want it to happen, I do not want to get out of my bed, I do not want it to be Christmas.

For a further hour, therefore, until the bells of St Thomas's church began to sound, Mrs Deirdre Fount slept.

In Birmingham on Christmas Eve, Aubrey Fount won a bottle of whisky in the staff raffle, and pinched the secretary to the Sales Manager on the way to their turkey and plum pudding in the staff canteen. At four o'clock the last post came and brought him a letter marked Personal.

Only a woman, thought Aubrey Fount, and only a woman like this one, would have been so cunning. She must have seen the address of the car showrooms on the disc inside the windscreen, and memorized it for just such an occasion.

'Dearest, dearest,' the letter began. Aubrey Fount felt depressed. He did not read it all, only enough to gather that she was trying to forgive him, trying to be hopeful, and understand. He could scarcely remember what she had looked like.

I would never blame you (wrote the girl Yvonne) because of course there must have been some very good reason for your leaving as you did, without letting me know. There – perhaps you *did* try to let me know, dear, and I am doing you an injustice. Oh, forgive me. What we both felt, so suddenly, must have been real and neither of us will be able to ignore it I am sure, or think of a future which does not include it. I am sure I cannot. It was the truth, Aubrey, do you not think so? People in this world find it so hard to communicate with one another, this sort of relationship happens so very rarely. So I am trying, you see, not to be at all anxious, just to sit quietly here and wait until I see or hear from you. But I cannot wait for *ever*, Aubrey.

Aubrey Fount sighed, and there floated into his mind a vision of all the other letters that would inevitably follow this one. He did not intend to reply but he knew that she would continue to write and the letters would grow more and more strident and desperate, until they started to accuse, as Yvonne lost hope and began to perceive the truth.

Well, he had tried to tell her, tried to teach her in that short time to be more sophisticated and mature about such a relationship, but it was all his own fault, he should have known better.

I will not be hounded, thought Aubrey Fount, taking a second tot of whisky, I will not be made to skulk and feel guilty by any woman.

Three days later, however, he got very drunk and proposed to Miriam, and when he was sober again he understood that she had at once accepted him. But at least it would solve the problem of the girl Yvonne.

In the Council Offices at Westbourne, Yvonne was being

kissed at the staff party by the man Clifford from the Borough Engineer's Department, and she spun round and slapped his face and made a scene.

'It was a joke,' he said, his neck flushing red with embarrassment, 'I was only being friendly. It's a party, it's Christmas.'

She had not heard him, for she had walked out in tears and got her coat and gone to lean over the railing of the Esplanade, looking down at the sea.

'Aubrey,' she said aloud, 'Aubrey, Aubrey.' She felt the tightness in her throat as she said his name and knew that it was love.

In the Council Offices, everybody began to dance.

Chapter Eleven

DEIRDRE FOUNT looked down at her new dress, laid out on the hotel bed, and remembered the only time she had bought clothes without consulting her mother. For they had always gone shopping together, and shared a changing room when both were buying. 'I know what suits you, Deirdre,' Mrs Winifred Oddicott would say, 'I have a good eye and you do not, you will try on something highly unsuitable and then allow yourself to be talked into buying it by some little shop girl.'

But this one time she had sneaked off to Hattersley and Porter's alone, to buy a dress for her honeymoon. If I do not begin now, to act by myself, make my own decisions, she had thought, I shall be lost once I am married. Not foreseeing that, even then, her mother would manage her life for her.

'I want something silky,' she had said to the girl, 'silky and patterned, and frivolous,' and she had bought exactly that, in pinks and purples, with a draped neckline. She had started off for home with the dress in its box and her heart beating with triumph and excitement, because the dress was her own purchase, her very own choice, and because when she wore it she would be a married woman. Her mother had had nothing to do with it. Though as she got nearer and nearer home, she began to have misgivings, for it was such a different type of dress and the colours were very dramatic. Perhaps she had not the presence to carry them off.

Mrs Oddicott had taken a single swift glance at it, pursed her lips and said nothing.

'Oh, mother, but it is a beautiful dress! Feel it, look at it. It is so soft and silky. I think it is very smart indeed, very *alluring*.'

Mrs Oddicott had turned and gone on with rolling out pastry, her back very straight.

Disappointment and resentment had welled up within

Deirdre Oddicott. What little assurance she had gained that afternoon was quite lost.

'Well *I* like it, and what is more, Aubrey will like it, and that is the important thing. So I do not care at all what *you* think.'

'But I have said nothing about it, Deirdre! I have not commented, not at all. You cannot accuse me of trying to influence you in any way. It is your dress and if you have bought it and are happy with it, then you must wear it, and I am sure nothing I might say would make the slightest difference. It has nothing to do with me.'

'No. No, it has not,' Deirdre Oddicott shouted in defiance, and gathered up the dress and its box, and took them upstairs to her room. But that evening, she had gone back and looked at it and known that she would never wear it.

'She wants to spoil everything for me,' she said at first, 'she is jealous because I have gone out on my own to buy it, she is jealous of everything I do these days, jealous that I am going to be married.'

But it was of no use, for her mother was right, the dress was awful, awful. She put it on and looked at herself in the long mirror and the purple and pink dress stood out so boldly that she herself faded away behind its colours, and the low neck hung down limply over her flat breasts. She had burst into tears of misery and frustration because everything had gone wrong and there was no hope for her. I am ugly, she said furiously, thin and plain and awkward, nice clothes do not suit me, the only things I do not look entirely foolish in are the things my mother selects, for she is right, she does know me best. That was the worst thing of all, knowing that her mother was right, because in her heart she felt sick with fear that Mrs Oddicott might be right about many other things.

Now, thirteen years later, she had once again gone into a shop alone and bought a dress. It is the start of my new life, she had said, and I shall wear what clothes *I* like, and every evening of this holiday, I shall change for dinner.

The dress was of silk jersey, in rather startling colours of turquoise and lime. Perhaps, she wondered now, she had been wrong to choose quite such bright shades, perhaps for her very first evening in the hotel it would be too conspicuous and in spite of the central heating she might be a little cold in short sleeves. The day after Boxing Day it had begun to snow.

Yet she was glad to have come here in the end, oh yes, for it was so very comfortable and they had seemed to go out of their way to make her welcome. There were log fires in all the public rooms and at five o'clock the maid had come round to draw the curtains and shut out the cold.

I shall have a long hot bath, said Deirdre Fount, and perhaps just for this evening put on the brown suit, until I have seen what other people are wearing.

But when she had done this, and combed her hair experimentally this way and that and fastened the single row of pearls about her neck and pinned the little mink brooch to her lapel, even then it was barely six o'clock. Dinner was not until seven-thirty. What shall I do, asked Mrs Deirdre Fount? Whatever shall I do with an hour and a half until the dinner gong, in a strange hotel and with no companion to talk to? For a moment, the next seven long, blank days stretched before her, with the snow outside and only four meals a day to look forward to.

But I am on holiday, she said firmly to herself, I am quite alone and I can please myself entirely, I may do this or that or just nothing at all. I can call my soul my own and how long is it since I had *that* opportunity? I have never been completely free in my life before. It is just that I shall have to learn to get used to it, I have started a little late and I must find many things to do, to fill my days.

She took a paperback novel about Tangiers, and her knitting and a new pad of writing paper, and went down into the lounge, where almost at once an elderly woman with brogues and a faint moustache started to talk to her about the weather.

There, thought Deirdre Fount, stretching her legs towards the fire, there, it is easy. Before I know where I am, I shall have made plenty of friends. Though she did not altogether like the idea of attaching herself so closely to other, solitary women, for it would make her look weak and unadventurous, she would be marked off at once as belonging with them. So she would be very polite but look around for other guests to talk to, younger people and married couples.

Meanwhile, as soon as she decently could, she said, 'Well, I have been very lucky indeed to snatch a day or so away like this. I have a son who is only eleven years old, I cannot often call my time my own.'

The grandfather clock in the hall struck six-fifteen.

In the end, Mrs Winifred Oddicott had to *ask* for a cup of tea.

'Of course I will make it myself,' she said to her niece Isobel. 'We will have one together. I do not expect you to wait on me – oh, no!' Though there has been no sign of any waiting, thought Mrs Oddicott, indeed, rather to the contrary. You take us as you find us, Isobel had said, and Mrs Oddicott was not sure that she approved of how she did find them, but it was not her place to say anything. She herself had always been brought up to believe that you made a little effort for your guests, baked extra cakes and set a bowl of flowers in their room, even brought them early morning tea once or twice. You must put them before yourself, her mother had always said, it is a case of F.H.B. – that had been her little phrase, Family Hold Back, and Mrs Oddicott was quite sure that her sister-in-law, Dora, had been the same and would have taught Isobel that way.

She filled the kettle and looked about for cups. 'I can manage perfectly,' she said, 'don't you trouble, I can just help myself.'

'I am afraid you will have to wash some. There don't seem to be any clean ones about, do there?'

'No, no,' said Mrs Winifred Oddicott, 'that's quite all right, don't trouble about me.'

At the kitchen table two of the boys sat with pots of glue and little brushes and models of aircraft in plastic.

'I suppose we all have our routines,' said Mrs Oddicott. 'We always have a cup of tea right after lunch, Deirdre and I. There is a kitchen behind the shop – so convenient. I think one misses these little things more than anything else.'

'Yes,' said Isobel.

'I would not like to interfere, dear, but I will just say that it would be a good idea if the boys had newspaper on the kitchen table, do you not agree? The glue, you see, it gets everywhere, you will be tasting it on the food. And it smells so.'

'Oh,' said Isobel, who was small and plump and young for her age, and was reading a magazine. 'Yes, I suppose it does.'

'Of course, James is only allowed messy things like glue and paint in his own room.'

'Poor old James,' said one of the boys, who looked exactly like his brother and was barely a year older, so that Mrs Oddicott had difficulty sorting out their names.

'Oh, James is a *very* happy boy, full of spirit. I am sure you would all get along splendidly.'

The boys looked at one another across the table and did not reply. Mrs Winifred Oddicott turned her attention back to the kettle. They are insolent, she decided, there is something insolent about their manner and expressions, though they do not actually *say* anything, there is nothing you could put your finger on and complain about. But I am very surprised for their father should know how to bring them up, as a school-master. It makes me appreciate James all the more, and I now realize that I have been a little unjust towards him recently. He may be quiet and reserved but that is no fault after all, and no one could call him insolent.

'If you have nothing to do, Aunty,' said Isobel, 'you could take the baby into the park, when you've had your tea.'

'Oh. Oh well, yes, dear. If you think he will be safe with me, if you feel I can manage.'

'Anybody,' said Isobel, stirring three lumps of sugar into her tea, 'can manage the baby. You could take Alexander as well actually. He quite likes you.'

Mrs Oddicott sipped her tea and said nothing, only thought of her daughter doing exactly as she pleased in a luxury hotel, and of James with the nice Schwartz family in Ross-shire. The moment you begin to grow old, she thought, your wishes start to be disregarded, you are no longer taken seriously or given any choice. It is a world run by the young for the benefit of themselves.

But in four days' time I shall be home again and then there will be a few changes. I shall leave Deirdre in the shop rather more and start to enjoy myself, visit my friends in Westbourne, go out here and there. But of course Isobel is being very kind in having me here and in a way I am grateful that they have not stood on ceremony but have straight away treated me as one of the family.

'We must wrap up warmly, dear,' she said, 'if we are to go out. It is bitterly cold.'

'Yes,' said Isobel vaguely, turning the page of her magazine, 'yes, I suppose it is.'

At lunch, Deirdre Fount noticed the man again. He was small, with rather sad, pouched eyes and a hesitant manner, but he wore a good suit and his hair was carefully cut. She herself tried to eat her meals in the hotel very slowly, to relax and look about her and smile at the waitress, for she noticed that all the other women bent their heads and rushed through their food, embarrassed at being alone.

The man ate turbot and helped himself to a lot of vegetables, and once he caught her eye as he darted little glances at people on the other tables, but before she had time to smile or bow, he looked away again. How sad, thought Deirdre Fount, how very sad for a man to be sitting alone. There is something very much more pathetic about a *man* without any companion. He was not old – perhaps fifty-five, she decided, and so, out of place in a hotel of this kind. For there were not, as she had hoped, any young people here at all.

The man ate hurriedly and was ill at ease. He had a sad, dull face and heavily pouched eyes, and Deirdre Fount was sorry for him, so that when they met afterwards in the lobby of the hotel she made a point of saying good evening. He looked at her in surprise.

'So cold now,' she said, 'it is a pleasure to stay in beside the fire.'

'Oh. Oh, yes. Yes indeed.'

But he did not venture to follow her into the lounge, where all the ladies were installed with their cups of coffee and romantic novels and knitting. It was exactly the same here as at Westbourne, Deirdre Fount saw, in the Majestic and the Regent and the Prince of Wales, and all the other private hotels along the Esplanade, where the elderly sat together in their favourite chairs and longed for the end of winter. God forbid, she thought, God forbid that I should come to that! And she wrapped herself up against the January cold and went for a brisk walk, down between the old stone houses as far as the river, thinking about James.

The following morning, in the parish church, she met the man again.

'The Church of St Cuthbert, Chinnington,' she read in the Leaflet for Visitors, 'is of Saxon foundation and the priest's doorway to the right of the Chancel remains in its original state. However, the building was partially destroyed by fire and rebuilt to the early Norman pattern, except for the Tower, which is of a later date.

'On the Chancel Floor may be seen the exceptionally fine brass memorial to Sir Lambert Hicks and his wife Angeline.'

Deirdre Fount walked up the aisle to look at the brass memorial. The man from the hotel was already there, holding a curious tweed hat.

'Oh,' said Mrs Fount, stopping short and giving a little laugh. 'Well what a coincidence! Good morning.'

He looked up and she saw at once that he was older than she had at first thought, he must be into his sixties, after all, though he looked well-preserved. There was a small spot of caked blood in the crease of his chin, from the morning's razor.

'I expect everyone finds their way to the church sooner or later,' she said, 'there are so many splendid features.'

'Oh, yes. Oh, quite.'

'What a noble bearing!' and she bent down to look more closely at the figure of Sir Lambert Hicks.

'He *is* very interesting. Yes, very fine.' Though he spoke uncertainly.

'Do you know much about brasses and that kind of thing? I daresay you do, but I confess that I am rather ignorant.'

'Not a great deal, I'm afraid. No. Not a great deal.'

They stared on at the memorial in silence for several more moments. Well, thought Deirdre Fount, so that is that. I have done my best to start a conversation, make him feel befriended, I had better move on. She walked vaguely in the direction of a reredos. 'Carved,' the Leaflet said, 'ornately.' But then she saw, 'dating from 1840' and lost interest. The church was very large, with pale windows and not much heating.

She heard the man say, 'It's a very comfortable hotel.' He was a few paces behind her, looking up at the carved screen. 'The last time I came down it was summer, we went out and about such a lot, you see, I suppose I scarcely noticed. But what with the weather and – and everything, I suppose you can judge a hotel by how you find it in winter.'

'Oh, I am sure you are right. I had not realized that you were a seasoned guest. I have never stayed here before, only been through the town, you know, some years ago.'

'I came with my wife,' the man said, and to the distress of Deirdre Fount his face suddenly crumpled with grief. 'Just a year ago this past summer. I came with my wife.'

'Oh. Oh, dear . . .'

His hands moved about inside the pockets of his overcoat. 'I thought it would be a good idea,' he said, 'a good thing, you see, to come back. But no. No, it isn't the same.'

'No,' said Deirdre Fount. 'No, of course.'

The cold church echoed with their voices.

'Do forgive me, Madam. I beg your pardon.'

'No, no. You should talk, you should never let things stay bottled up, I am sure people have told you that before. It is always best to talk and *I* do not mind, not at all.'

'How kind,' he murmured, 'very kind.'

'You will be feeling very much alone.'

'My sister warned me, you know, she told me that it was unwise. You will remember everything, Arthur, she said, it will all come flooding back. But I thought that I would *like* to remember that happy time, you see, I thought I was sufficiently recovered and I could think all about her again. I did need a holiday . . .'

They had begun to walk slowly towards the door and Deirdre Fount wanted to say yes, yes, do not upset yourself, I understand, you can tell everything to me. Aloud, however, she only said, 'My name is Fount. Mrs Deirdre Fount.'

'Smithers, Arthur Smithers.'

They stopped, just beside the Missionary Society Bookstall, and shook hands.

'There is something wrong with my stomach,' said Major Bertram Carpenter. Mrs Carpenter sighed, wishing that he would not always begin to complain about himself late at night, when she was tired, for then she would lie awake and worry and feel ill herself, the following day.

'Did you hear what I said, Flora?'

'Yes, I heard, dear, but if it is your indigestion again . . .'

'I did not say that I was in pain, I said that there was something wrong. There *is* something wrong.'

He stood in the centre of the room, his left hand flat on his stomach just above the navel, feeling about carefully.

'There is a swelling,' he said, 'it feels peculiar, hard and tight.'

'I expect you have wind, dear. It is just the same with babies, you know, they have these griping pains and their little stomachs are like footballs, and it is all because of wind. The same with you.'

'What nonsense, Flora! I am not a baby, there can be no comparison.'

'Oh, we are all made very much alike,' said Mrs Carpenter, because it seemed the best way, to treat these recent symptoms of her husband as lightly as she could. He was becoming a hypochondriac, he spent much of his time buying and taking different patent medicines and fussing about his food, and feeling his stomach.

'I did not realize until now,' he said bitterly, 'that I had married an unsympathetic woman. It has taken illness, real illness for me to understand that you do not care.'

And he sat down miserably on the bed, his hands held against him.

'Now you know that is not true, Bertram, you know it is quite unjust. I have all the sympathy in the world with you and indeed, with all pain and suffering, however trivial.'

'This is not *trivial*.'

'I am not saying so. But there is a limit to my patience, dear, for if you will not see a doctor, what more do you expect me to do?'

Major Carpenter thought for a moment and then said, 'What do you suppose that a doctor would do?'

'He would examine you, find out the cause of all this indigestion, that is what he would do.'

'I will not go near any hospital, Flora. I have given you plenty of warning about that. I will not go and endure all manner of unpleasant tests. I know these hospitals, I have seen what goes on. Once you are inside a hospital you are a dead man.'

Oh, how many times, thought Mrs Carpenter, how many times? For I have heard it all before.

'Doctor Rogers would never send you to a hospital against your will. He *could* not do so and besides I am quite sure there will be no need, it will all be settled after five minutes in his surgery.'

Major Carpenter got into bed and for a long time, almost half an hour, he lay with his hands resting on his distended stomach, and his eyes wide open, looking into the darkness.

'Well,' he said at last, as his wife was almost asleep. 'You had better telephone the man tomorrow, you had better make an appointment.'

'Oh yes, dear! Of course I will. Oh, I am sure you have made the right decision, I will ring him first thing in the morning. Doctor Rogers will have you better in no time, you will see.'

Major Carpenter grunted. But in the night he tossed and tossed and dreamed of hospitals, and saw his friend Isepp's dying face, the colour of a bad mushroom, bobbing up and down like a lifebuoy, far out to sea.

When he awoke, his stomach no longer felt hard and tight, the indigestion was quite gone, and he decided that there was no need to see the doctor. But it was five minutes to nine, the tea tray had arrived and in the sitting room, Mrs Flora Carpenter was already on the telephone.

'Well, I will go,' said her husband, 'I will go to keep you happy, Flora. Remember that, please, it is only to keep you happy.'

'Yes, dear,' said Mrs Flora Carpenter.

'*She* has not lost any time in finding a gentleman friend,' said one of the ladies to another, in the lounge of the Phoenix House Hotel.

'This morning, my dear, I saw that they were sharing a table for coffee in the Tudor Rooms.'

'Yet she seemed so friendly at first, so eager to talk to all of us.'

'Until Mr Smithers arrived.'

And several others turned to watch him get out of his car and enter the hotel with Mrs Deirdre Fount.

Though it had been quite accidental about the coffee, for he had already been seated there, fumbling helplessly with the hot silver handles when Deirdre Fount arrived. It would, she thought later, have looked very rude and rather self-conscious of her to sit alone at another table, even though he had seemed just a little startled when she had joined him. A lady, Mrs Winifred Oddicott would have said, waits to be asked.

I will draw him out, thought Deirdre Fount, get him to talk about himself and his interests. It is not good for a man to sit and brood alone over the memory of a dead wife.

Already she was feeling better about the holiday, she seemed to have got into the stride of it and the days were quickly over. Each evening she wore the dress of turquoise and lime green silk jersey and ignored the disapproving glances of the other women. Why, they are jealous, she said to herself, looking around the dining room, they see that I am still quite young and know how to make the most of company, they see that I have made a friend of Mr Smithers, and so I am resented. How very silly! As if there were anything at all unsuitable about such a thing.

'My sister is very good to me,' Arthur Smithers had said. 'My sister Marjorie. She has – well, made a new home for me, you see, these last eighteen months. I have a lot to thank her for.'

'Yes,' said Deirdre Fount. 'Yes. How kind!'

Though was there not some blame to be attached to a sister who had let him come away, unhappy as he was, all alone?

'Marjorie was a nurse, a State Registered Nurse, before her marriage. She was very competent, I believe. She is a widow now, of course, such as yourself.'

'Oh, but *I* am not a widow,' said Deirdre Fount quickly, before she could ask herself whether it was a good idea. 'No, no. I have been divorced.'

One or two people in the lounge had glanced up, and then at one another discreetly. Now, they thought, *now* we understand, now her behaviour is abundantly clear. But Mr Smithers did not seem to mind, did not comment in any way. He only said, 'You will be pleased to have your son, he will be something for you to be proud of.'

Deirdre Fount settled back happily to tell him a great deal about James.

As Mr Arthur Smithers was dropping his dentures into the effervescent cleanser later that night, he remembered what his sister Marjorie had said.

Not that he had taken any notice of it at the time.

'You will have to be very careful, Arthur, now that you are a widower again and a man of some means. You will be a sitting target for all sorts of grabbing women. You know how weak you are, how easily you can be made to feel sorry for anyone at all and how eager for company. That is the reason I do not think you should go on holiday alone. Take a friend, if you do not care to take me. Take your cousin Harold.'

But Arthur Smithers had not liked the idea of going on a holiday with another man, nor did he care much for his cousin Harold. He had been very firm about wanting this week quite alone.

Of course it had not been right, it had only reminded him of how inadequate he was and how much he missed Amy. He had been very glad to talk to the nice Mrs Fount. She is not a grabbing female, he thought, surely Marjorie would not disapprove of her? But he was a little uneasy, all the same, for there was something about her, just something . . .

He got in between the tight-fitting sheets and thought again of Amy and how she had been so happy buying little presents for everyone in the Gifts and Crafts shop, and cutting into a different kind of cake every day at the Tudor Rooms.

'It's a treat,' she had kept on saying to him, 'it is one long treat, Arthur.' Because she had been so very ill, he had not expected to take her away, and see her so cheerful and fit ever again. It had all been too good to be true.

Mr Arthur Smithers lay upon his back in the hotel bed and wept, as he had wept for so many nights since the death of Amy. Really, he thought, there is no point in staying here, none at all, there is nothing for me to enjoy, nobody whose company I really want. I had better go back home to Marjorie.

*

'Oh!' said Mrs Deirdre Fount, 'Oh, what has happened? Whatever can be wrong?'

For there was Mr Arthur Smithers at the reception desk, writing out a cheque, and his bags stood beside him on the floor.

'You are surely not leaving today?'

'Ah – ah, Mrs Fount. I am glad you have come, glad you have caught me, before ... Yes, I am going back home, I have telephoned to my sister and it is all arranged.'

'Your sister is ill then? You have been forced to cut short your holiday. Oh ...'

'No, no.' Mr Smithers accepted his receipted bill and tucked it away in his wallet, looking embarrassed. 'It is not that, nothing is wrong with anyone. Except me, I daresay, Mrs Fount, except me.'

'*You* are ill?'

'No. But it was not such a good idea to come, I have decided – you will understand. I have walked about this town and remembered and it has done me no good.'

'Oh,' said Deirdre Fount. 'Oh, yes. Of course.'

'My sister was right. I will be better off quietly at home.'

'Yes.'

'But I am glad to have met you, glad that you could find time for our little chats.'

'I could not ...'

'Yes?'

'Well – no, nothing. Nothing.'

'Ah. Now I shall go and see about getting out my car.'

Goodbye, she was about to say, goodbye Mr Smithers, if you feel that you do not want to stay here, that I am not enough to keep you from your sister, goodbye, and she would shake hands formally, hiding her disappointment in him. But the girl at the reception desk was touching her elbow.

'Mrs Fount? I am sorry to interrupt. There is a telephone call for you from Edinburgh.'

When she turned round again, Mr Smithers had picked up his luggage and gone out of the hotel door.

Mrs Winifred Oddicott thought that she had never known it to be so cold, never in her life before, as she trailed round the dismal little park with the baby in a pushchair and Alexander, who kept running away into the bushes, and the dog called Angus, on a long, awkward lead. There are only two more days to go, she thought, but I can bear it no longer, I will pack my bags and go home tonight, invent some excuse, for they are simply making use of me, I am quite worn out. While she endured the cold and the naughtiness of Alexander, her niece read magazines in front of the fire.

I wish that I had never given in to Deirdre, I wish that I had had the sense to remain at home. It was only done to please her, and she will never be grateful, it was done to make her feel that I was being looked after, to stop her worrying about me. If, indeed, that is what she would have done.

There is the Christmas window display still to be dismantled and the Sale Goods to sort out and mark, I could have gone about things at my own pace and had everything well in hand. When they saw that I was there by myself I am sure the people of Westbourne would have invited me out, for I am not without my friends, whatever Deirdre may think. Well, this has taught me a lesson, I shall not give in to her again. When I get home I shall be able to make her feel ashamed of the time I have had here, and she must hear me out, for I have been silent and patient with her long enough, I do not intend to go on letting matters slide.

They had reached the gates of the park.

'Lolly,' said the three-year-old Alexander, 'lolly now,' because there was the painted cart standing across the street.

'No, you may not have a lollipop,' said Mrs Winifred Oddicott, 'you are a greedy little boy and it will chill your stomach in this terrible weather. When we get home you shall have your nice tea.'

'Lolly,' said Alexander, and started forward suddenly, out of her grasp and across the road.

Mrs Oddicott released her hold on the baby's pram and the dog and stumbled, shouting in anger, after Alexander. She looked for traffic to the right of her, but not to the left.

'Oh dear God!' said Deirdre Fount, and her feet were suddenly very unsteady on the ground, the telephone receiver went heavy in her hand.

'Dear God!'

'Mrs Fount? Sit down here, look. I have brought you a chair. Are you going to be all right?'

The voice of the desk girl came and went, loud and then faint by turns, and at the other end of the telephone receiver, Mrs Oddicott's niece Isobel stammered on.

'You had better come,' she was saying, 'isn't that best? You had better come up to Edinburgh tonight.'

Chapter Twelve

'TAKE a deep breath,' said Doctor Rogers.

'Thank you. And another . . .

'Another . . .'

'It is my *stomach*,' said Major Bertram Carpenter, 'there is nothing wrong with my lungs.'

'Another deep breath, please.'

And in their suite at the Prince of Wales Hotel, Mrs Flora Carpenter waited anxiously, for he had insisted on going alone. 'I am not a child,' he had said, 'I do not need you to come and hold my hand.'

Let it be nothing, let there be nothing seriously wrong, she thought now, as she stood by the wide window and looked out to sea. He has always been such a healthy man, until that awful bronchitis last winter at least, he is not used to sickness and the ways of doctors, he would not know how to cope. Women are so much more able to accept and overcome these things, we are never so vulnerable.

Doctor Rogers moved his hands to right and left over the surface of the stomach.

'You have a fairly light touch,' said Major Carpenter. 'I am feeling no discomfort, I will say that for you.'

Doctor Rogers nodded. 'How long has this been troubling you, Major? Very long?'

'Since our return from the West Indies, several weeks ago. We cruised, you know, and I was perfectly all right then, no matter what I ate and drank. It began upon our return. I thought they were poisoning my food, I can tell you.'

Doctor Rogers did not smile. 'Any pain?'

'Pain? Well, of course I have pain, I have described it all to you. I lie awake every night with the pain.'

'But that is indigestion, discomfort, a feeling of fullness, or however you may like to describe it. I am talking about real sharp pain.'

'I would like to describe *this* as "real sharp pain", I thank you,' said Major Carpenter.

'Sit up now, put on your jacket, Major. I have quite finished.'

'So now you will give me a bottle of some medicine or other, and let us hope it is of more use than all that other stuff I have been drinking.'

'I rather wish that you had not done that, I would have preferred to see you earlier. It is never a good idea to dose oneself when symptoms persist.'

He talks like a bank manager, thought Major Carpenter, he has a sour expression, there is no humanity in him.

'I do not like the medical profession,' he said. 'I may as well be frank with you. It is only for the sake of my wife, only to keep her happy and stop her worrying, that I am here at all.'

'Yes, yes.'

'Well, get on with your writing, give me the form for the chemist and I can be on my way.'

'I am going to make an appointment for you to see a consultant, Major Carpenter, that is what I am writing now. I want you to visit the hospital.'

Afterwards, Mrs Deirdre Fount said to a number of people, 'I know that I shall never in my life experience such a terrible journey again.' For it was like a nightmare that might never end. The compartment of the train was full and so hot that she felt she might no longer be able to breathe, but outside in the corridor there had simply been no heating at all. It was not an express train but stopped at every possible station, and was held up from time to time: it grew dark early, so that she could only stare at her own reflection in the window. She had brought no book, only a newspaper, and that was quickly read. Nobody sitting in her compartment wanted to begin a conversation and although she would not, she felt, have been able to make much effort, a little sympathy and attention would have drawn her out and comforted her.

Beyond Carlisle it began to snow, and she thought of James, standing about on the open platforms of railways, catching a chill. I should never have let him go, they must be a very casual family, and he has no woman with him to see to these little things. Men do not have very much common sense of that kind. Besides, I need to know exactly where he is, even to have him with me at a time like this.

Until she gathered her senses and realized that it was probably a great deal of panic about nothing, that her journey might well be unnecessary. It was so like Mrs Oddicott to call for her, insist that she cut short the one holiday she had been able to take since her honeymoon thirteen years before. If Mr Arthur Smithers had not been rushing away so suddenly that morning, she would not have felt so bad, for she might have asked him to be of some help. But it was almost as though he had tried to avoid her that morning, to get away without being seen.

Well, thought Mrs Deirdre Fount, I am sure I did not behave improperly, I cannot think what he should suspect me of. I was trying to befriend him kindly, to make his holiday a little less lonely, that is all.

In a way she was relieved to have left the Phoenix House Hotel, for the ladies would sit by the fire that evening and speculate about the departure of Mr Smithers, and if she had been there Deirdre Fount would have been forced to talk to them again, or else to sit alone in her bedroom, waiting for the gong. The holiday, she knew now, had not been a good idea, she had been lonely and miserable and self-conscious without any companion, she had hated the meals alone and the chintzy curtains and the other solitary women. Nevertheless, she knew also that when her mother asked her, she would talk about the lovely scenery and the home cooking and her new friend, the charming Mr Smithers. 'I intend to take just such another holiday again, mother,' she decided to say, 'it has given me a taste for freedom.'

When she got out of the train at Edinburgh the cold made her draw in her breath suddenly, and then, there was a man in a grey duffle coat who introduced himself as Murray, the husband of Isobel.

'Yes, I am Mrs Fount,' she said briskly. 'How do you do? And you cannot imagine how glad I am to get off that appalling train!'

He was a huge man, with thick, ungloved hands. 'I am sorry you had to come all this way,' he said, 'but perhaps . . . perhaps you . . . but Mrs Oddicott is dead.'

'I told you but you would have none of it, you would not listen to me, Flora. *I* told you how it would be. But I walked out, I was not going to listen to more, I simply walked out and I do not intend to go back. Now I warn you not to start nagging and trying to persuade me, because the matter is at an end, I am not going near any hospital.'

'Oh dear,' said Mrs Flora Carpenter.

'Yes, you may well look distressed, Flora. *I* have been distressed, I may tell you, I have spent a most unpleasant and disturbing afternoon, the very smell of that surgery and the sight of all those gadgets and instruments brought it back to me, the way my poor friend Isepp went. Well, that is that, and now I would be glad if you would ring down for some tea.'

'But he did not say *why* he wanted you to see a consultant, Bertram. Did he not explain what he thought might be wrong with you?'

'He did not, I did not give the man a chance.'

Mrs Carpenter stood up suddenly and faced her husband. 'If you refuse to be examined further,' she said in a very quiet voice, 'you may become seriously ill, it may go from bad to worse with you.'

'Nonsense.'

'Oh, it is easy to say nonsense, but you do not know.'

'These fellows all make work for one another, Flora, it is a question of jobs for the boys. They pass their patients on like so many buckets of water in a fire chain and each doctor on the way collects a fat fee. At the end of it all you are given a clean bill of health, it has been a fuss and an expense for nothing.'

'Well . . .'

'Now have I not said that I do not want an argument? The subject is closed.'

Mrs Flora Carpenter set her lips very tightly together. 'Very well, Bertram,' she said, and picked up the telephone to ask for a tray of tea. 'Very well.'

But she could not rest, could not leave the matter there, for she was his wife, and anxious about him, it was her duty to see him well. In the night she lay awake and heard him tossing and she was suddenly afraid.

The following morning Major Carpenter went out to Boots the Chemists and bought two large bottles of a new patent medicine.

'I am very surprised that Doctor Rogers did not give you anything,' said his wife. Major Carpenter did not reply.

'So you are still having pain?'

'We will not talk about it, if you please, Flora. I will take this and I have no doubt that it will do the trick, the pharmacist gave it a strong recommendation. I shall be quite better in no time.'

He went to get a wine-glassful of water in which to mix his first tablespoon of medicine.

Mrs Flora Carpenter waited until five minutes past two, when he was settled on the settee with cushions for his afternoon nap. He slept every day now, solidly from two until four.

I shall go and see Doctor Rogers, she decided, I shall ask him straight out and get to the bottom of all this, I shall discover the truth, for it is best that I should know.

'I have to apologize,' she began by saying, once within the surgery, 'for my husband. He is not always in the best of tempers.'

'He has a poor opinion of doctors, certainly.'

'Yes, and I am very much afraid you will never alter it, his mind is quite made up. It is too late for putting forward reasonable arguments and too late for coaxing and persuasion.'

'He does not make things easy for himself. He ought to be seen by a specialist at the hospital, Mrs Carpenter.'

'He will never go near any hospital.'

'If he comes here for my advice and treatment, and then refuses to accept . . .'

'Doctor Rogers,' said Mrs Flora Carpenter, drawing herself up very straight in the uncomfortable chair, 'I beg you will tell me *your* opinion, tell me what you believe is the truth. I have a right to know, and that is not something I often claim.'

'Major Carpenter has complained of indigestion.'

'There is more to it than that, he is a sensible eater and he has never suffered from anything of that kind in the whole of his life before.'

'Quite.'

'What is wrong, Doctor Rogers?'

'I do not know. That is why I have suggested a visit to the hospital. I would like to find out, so that any treatment which . . .'

'To find out *what*? What is it that you suspect, Doctor?'

Doctor Rogers tapped the end of his silver pencil on the desk. Here is a determined woman, he thought, a woman of courage. Perhaps, after all, I would do best to respect it and to tell her what I may have found. But they are both old and would it not be kinder to keep them in ignorance, let nature take its course, jolly them along and talk of some other, more trivial possibility?

Mrs Carpenter wore a fur coat, very old-fashioned in style and too long for her, but a mink coat, and the brooch on the collar of her dress beneath was a hoop of diamonds. She is well provided for, he thought, well protected. At least she will never be faced with the hardships brought about by illness and poverty together. Her skin was clear and fine, the bones of her nose and cheeks most delicate. She has been a beautiful woman, thought Doctor Rogers.

'I think that your husband has cancer,' he told her.

'Yes,' said Mrs Carpenter, 'yes, that is what I thought.'

'Then you will understand that his condition should be diagnosed for certain without any delay, so that, if I am right, we may begin treatment.'

'Major Carpenter will never put up with any treatment, he will not have anything to do with other doctors, specialists and hospitals. Can you not understand that?'

'If he does not . . .'

'Yes. But then, he is not a young man, Doctor Rogers, and what chance is there that he will recover, even after all your treatment? I am well informed, you must not try to pull the wool over my eyes.'

'I think he may be no better after treatment, Mrs Carpenter, I think it may be too late, the cancer may be in the wrong place, and he is not, as you have said, a young man. But I have said, *I think*, I do not know. And there is a good chance, because there is always a chance, these matters are never predictable. I have seen men older than the Major and apparently hopeless cases undergo serious operations and make a complete recovery. If there is a chance of life who am I – who are *you* – to deny him that? *If* I am right in suspecting what I do. At the moment it is all hypothesis.'

Mrs Flora Carpenter rose, holding the mink coat high against her throat.

'Thank you,' she said, and made a little bow across the desk. 'Thank you, Doctor Rogers.'

She walked to the door of the consulting room.

'And are you going to tell your husband what I have said? Will you try and *frighten* him into going to see a consultant?'

'I do not know what I shall do,' said Mrs Carpenter. And left.

But that is not true, she thought, walking along the cold Esplanade towards the bandstand and the putting green. I do know, I have known from the beginning, because this is what I suspected and I have been thinking about it constantly. Nevertheless, I will think about it some more, I will go and sit in the primrose gardens and think until I am quite sure in my mind. But I know already.

There were just four of them in the enormous car: Deirdre Fount, Isobel and Isobel's husband Murray, and Isobel's mother, Mrs Oddicott's sister-in-law Dora, from Preston.

These people, thought Deirdre Fount, are 'family' yet I do not know them at all, they have never had anything to do with us, it might just as well be a group of strangers at my mother's funeral.

In front of them the hearse was now empty except for the bearers. It was a long way back from the crematorium to the house.

I should have had her taken home after all, thought Deirdre Fount. There she would have been surrounded by friends, the people of Westbourne would have rallied round and filled the church for her funeral, and I would have felt better, knowing that she was going to rest in her own home town. But the decision had been made in such a hurry and she had been confused. Everyone else had said that this was the best, the most sensible way. 'Such an expense,' they all said, 'so unnecessary, really.' 'She would never have wanted it.'

But I am the only one who can know what she would have wanted and I have gone against it. For she had known, the moment she entered Isobel's house, that Mrs Oddicott would have hated it here, where everything was untidy and disorganized, where the furniture was modern and the children impolite. She would not have wanted a funeral and cremation in that city.

'There are your mother's things,' said Isobel, leading her up to the little bedroom. 'Perhaps you would . . .?'

Whatever I may be going to feel, Deirdre Fount had thought, looking down at the small brown suitcase and the petit-point hairbrush and the navy blue jersey suit, whatever it is, I will not feel it yet. I am not going to think about it or brood or let myself go in this house. I must be controlled and businesslike, for it will soon be over and I shall be home. But her immediate feeling had been one of liberation, and she was ashamed of it. Although, given our relationship over the past few months, she thought, it is only to be expected. Is it surprising that, for the first time in my whole life, I feel free rather than bereaved?

Mrs Oddicott's niece Isobel and her husband Murray seemed only to be concerned about the child Alexander. His mother watched him and took him on to her knee and talked about him incessantly.

'He is not yet four,' she said, cutting herself a mid-morning slice of cake. 'To have seen all that, to have seen the lorry and heard all the dreadful noises and have to be taken off with the baby and the dog by a policeman!'

'He will never forget it,' said Aunt Dora, 'it will always leave a scar.'

'I shall have to be very careful with him. I do not think we shall ever be able to go into that park again.'

But it was *my* mother who was killed, thought Deirdre Fount, my mother. She held up the navy blue suit. 'I wondered, Aunt Dora . . . Perhaps . . .? It will not do for me, of course, and it seems such a waste to carry everything home . . .'

Aunt Dora took the jacket and held it up against herself. 'She wore that,' said Isobel, 'just the morning before. Only it was too cold, she said, too cold to go out in. So she changed.'

Deirdre Fount turned away.

The wrought-iron bandstand was empty of chairs and rostrum for the winter months and a tarpaulin covered the floor. Mrs Flora Carpenter sat alone on one of the recessed seats in the primrose gardens and looked up at it and thought of the summer, when the players would reassemble and there would be music and her husband might be dead.

If I tell him what may be wrong, she thought, he will at first refuse to believe me. But he will brood about it and in time, when the symptoms do not go but only worsen, he will realize the truth and begin to be afraid. He will never agree to visit the hospital except perhaps when it is far too late, and even supposing that he *were* to be persuaded, what would it be for him but weeks and months of unpleasant treatment, perhaps even an operation? He would be very weak and might be no better at the end of it all. But if he does not know, the illness will simply take its course and that course may be a slow one, perhaps even fairly painless, and he will have nothing to fear, he will know nothing. I will nurse him myself in our own room at the hotel, there will be no need for doctors and hospitals if I can help it.

Yes, there is no doubt in my mind, for that is what he would want. I know my own husband after all these years.

At her feet a robin hopped about, looking for crumbs or a worm, but when she moved, flew up into the leafless hedge.

And what of me, thought Mrs Carpenter? If Bertram is to die, what shall I do, for I cannot remember a time without him, and he is my husband, however difficult he may have been these past few months, I cannot think what my life will be like without him. Only I shall never let myself go, I shall not mourn and be a burden to everyone, I shall not sit back and wait for senility and death. If I am to be left alone, I shall take myself in hand, I shall see to it that I have a positive future, not a mere existence.

He is waiting for me at the hotel, and I have always told him everything, there have been no secrets between us until now. I cannot tell him this, that is what I have decided, but I must tell someone, it will be more of a strain than I can bear to keep all this knowledge and responsibility to myself. I shall ring Edward – yes, for he has a right to know.

A great wave crashed up against the sea wall, sending a sheet of pale foam up and over, and in the primrose garden Mrs Carpenter felt some of the fine spray on her face. I am getting old, she thought, and tired, the winter exhausts me, and the spring and summer will bring nothing to look forward to. She stood up. And was at once ashamed of herself. A *positive future*, she said aloud. I am seventy-one and I have my health and faculties, I live an easy and comfortable life in a pleasant town, there are many people who would envy me. And after all, Doctor Rogers may be quite wrong, Bertram may be alive and well in ten years time, it is all hypothesis and suspicion.

But I will telephone to Edward. I will tell him, just in case.

At twenty minutes to nine, Major Bertram Carpenter came back from the Conservative Club to the Prince of Wales Hotel. He had hoped to find friends but he had stayed three quarters of an hour and no friend had come. 'It is the winter,' the secretary had said, 'the bad weather keeps our older members away.'

'It has not kept me away,' said Major Carpenter. 'They have no courage, no fighting spirit. They sit at home with shawls and hot-water bottles, martyrs to old age.'

Though since last winter several had died and now Isepp was gone, and it was not the same. Major Carpenter had come away. I still have plenty of energy left, he said, plenty of attack, there is precious little wrong with *me*. And he walked up all the floors instead of taking the hotel lift. Outside the door, he stopped, hearing voices.

Now this is annoying, thought Major Carpenter, Flora has invited some visitor or other and they are sitting in there chattering and I shall be forced to listen. She made no mention of it to me, thinking, I daresay, that she would have the evening to herself, the coast quite clear. It will be some woman or other whom she has met in the lounge.

He put his hand on the door.

'Doctor Rogers is very good,' his wife was saying. He stopped and listened. 'Of course he could not say without the benefit of hospital tests and . . . no, no, of course . . . but that is the trouble, Edward . . . Yes. *He* thinks it is cancer, and so I thought that you should know . . . I beg your pardon?'

Major Bertram Carpenter closed the door again and retreated into the long, empty hotel corridor.

At the other end of the telephone line, Edward Carpenter was talking about the need to *insist* upon tests and the opinion of other doctors, the foolishness of this and that, he was saying, 'I think you are quite wrong, mother, I think he should be told. Apart from anything else, it will bring him to his senses.'

Mrs Carpenter listened sadly. But I have made up my mind, she thought, for I am the one who knows him best, *I* am the one to decide.

I am all alone, thought Mrs Deirdre Fount, looking round the empty kitchen. For it was in the kitchen, where Mrs Oddicott had so often been, that she felt worst of all. She walked about it uncertainly, touching a plate and a pan and the edge of the gas cooker. I do not really know how to cook, she said, I left all that to her, and what little I had to do after I married is now all forgotten. She did not like me to interfere and now I must take down the cookery books and somehow learn by trial and error, for James has to be fed.

James Fount was now upstairs, sorting out his railway post-cards before his cases were even fully unpacked. He had said nothing about his grandmother and Deirdre Fount had no idea what he might be thinking.

'Oh, there is so much to be done,' she had said to Isobel, 'I shall have no time to brood and fret, none at all.'

Now she looked about her and thought of it all, the decisions that would have to be made about the shop and the house and Mrs Oddicott's belongings. They are all *my* decisions, thought Deirdre Fount, nobody can make them for me, there is nobody to help me, nobody upon whom to lean. I am quite alone. I have no father, brother or husband to support and advise me, only an eleven-year-old son.

But this is what I wanted, my freedom and independence, the opportunity to choose and decide, this is what I have always longed for. She remembered the day she had sat in the rose gardens and seen the awful, restricted future stretching ahead of her to the grave, without hope or opportunity or change. Now that will never be, she thought, now I can do what I please for the rest of my life.

Mrs Deirdre Fount sat down on the plastic-topped kitchen stool and wept.

In his room, James Fount counted what was left of the holiday money to see if he had enough to buy a large scrap album for the postcards. There was two and ninepence. That afternoon he would go to Schwartz's house and they would start to classify the loco numbers and take in their colour slides to be developed.

'My grandmother is dead,' he had said, and Mrs Schwartz had looked upset and offered him chocolates for comfort.

'But she was quite old.'

Once or twice he had woken in the night and thought about Mrs Oddicott lying injured in the roadside, and been both frightened and distressed. She will not be here any more, he had told himself, I will never, never see her again. But after that, he had tried not to think about it.

Dear Aubrey [wrote Mrs Deirdre Fount],

I am sure you will be very shocked and sorry to hear that my mother died last week, after a road accident in Edinburgh. I was alone on holiday in the Cotswolds and had to travel up there to see to everything; the funeral and cremation were in Scotland. James was also in Scotland, having a holiday with a school friend and his family, but we are both home now and he starts school this week.

I am finding it very hard to think just what to do for the best, Aubrey, about my own future and James's. That is why I am writing to you, I do so feel in need of your advice. You are James's father, after all, that is the only reason I feel it right to call on you.

I have seen the solicitor and my mother was comfortably provided for, but I do not know what to do about the shop or whether to stay here and keep James at Westbourne Priors School, manage the shop as best I can myself. Or should I take a chance and make a clean break, start a new life for James and myself? I am still young enough, after all.

I would not like to uproot James, though, or to do anything without consulting you and especially since you showed that you were so interested in him, by coming up here before Christmas. My mother would never like us to have any bad feeling in the family.

I am finding it very lonely here, and I am still suffering badly from shock so that if things do not get better I feel I may break down in some way. But of course I will put on a cheerful face, for James. He is being very quiet and he has said so little about his grandmother that I am beginning to get rather anxious. I would not like to think of him bottling up his grief. But he is very young and perhaps does not realize it fully.

It would be a great help if you would write to me, Aubrey, or even come here for a weekend. I need to feel that someone is behind me. Otherwise I would not have written. It is really for James's sake, not for myself.

Mrs Deirdre Fount walked along the Esplanade after posting the letter to Birmingham. On the roof-tops of the Regency crescent, the snow lay in little broken piles – waiting, Mrs Winifred Oddicott would have said, for some more to come and take it away.

It was Sunday afternoon.

Up in the sitting room of her balcony flat, Miss Violet Prug ate a crystallized fruit and looked down on the Esplanade.

'Oh dear,' she said to her companion, 'now there is poor Deirdre Fount.'

'Coming here?'

'No, no. Walking along and staring at the sea.'

'What a shock for her – what a terrible shock!'

Mrs Christie was re-hemming a linen napkin.

'I suppose we should invite her up. We will have to make some kind of an effort, for she will be feeling very much alone just now.'

'She has always been dominated by her mother, she will be quite at a loss.'

'I will write to her, ask her to tea or supper.'

'But there is the boy . . .'

'Lunch, then, while the boy is at school. Yes. It will take her out of herself.'

Miss Prug took another crystallized fruit. 'And there,' she said after a moment, 'is Major Carpenter stumping along and looking as bad tempered as ever.'

'I think that he leads *Mrs* Carpenter a very difficult life.'

The rich Miss Prug watched Mrs Fount and the Major come towards one another and pass, without pause or recognition. She was a little surprised.

'But the Carpenters are together,' she said to Mrs Christie, 'they do have one another.'

And she watched the solitary figure of Deirdre Fount in her long, old-fashioned coat, as she walked slowly out of sight round the curve of the Esplanade.

Major Bertram Carpenter stopped and rested his hands on the cold railings, standing very straight.

It is a pack of lies, he had told himself ever since Friday night, Doctor Rogers is a fool and an alarmist, I will believe none of it, it cannot possibly be true.

But he had thought about it for two days and now it was Sunday and he knew that it must be true. I have a feeling, he would have said to his friend Isepp, I have a feeling. For he could have told Isepp and been happier in his mind, Isepp had known what was what.

Major Carpenter watched the lifebuoy that marked the war-time wreck, two miles out. I shall not tell Flora, he thought, she will never know that I have heard her conversation. I have waited, given her plenty of opportunity to tell me about it but she has not, she has gone about the hotel with a cheerful face, talking of trivialities. She is keeping it from me. Edward is to know but I am not. Very well, I shall not know, I shall carry on just as before, and Flora will have her way, it can do me no harm to indulge her. And if they are all proved wrong, if they are waiting for me to sicken and die, and I do not . . .

He leaned harder on the railings and was suddenly afraid. Isepp is dead, thought Major Carpenter, I watched him die and nothing could be done for him and now it is my turn, I am to go. Well, it was all very well for Isepp, for he was unconscious at his death, *he* overheard nothing, nobody spoke the truth, and he died in happy ignorance. I shall not. But Flora is a woman, she is my wife and must be protected. So long as I have made it abundantly clear that I will never go into a hospital, so long as that is understood.

Walking back up Pavilion Terrace, Mrs Deirdre Fount thought, that was Major Carpenter, an acquaintance even if not a close friend and he walked straight past me, cut me dead. This town is full of people well known to me, customers at the shop, those who would come in and chat to my mother, tell her all their troubles, but since my return, I have seen no one, they are oblivious to any needs but their own.

Tomorrow, I must open the shop alone, and organize the Sale items, start to make decisions about the future. I have no reason whatsoever to stay in Westbourne, said Deirdre Fount, it is a town of old, selfish and dying people, they mean nothing to me at all. I ought to make a fresh start, go to some large city among new, younger people. For Westbourne does not care. My mother is not here to overrule me, I do not have to feel tied to her and dependent upon her, nor need I worry about being responsible for her in her declining years. Many women would envy me. By staying in this place of old age and retirement I can do myself nothing but harm.

She began to walk up the avenue towards her own house with a very determined step.

'My grandmother has been killed,' said James Fount. For he had discovered that it gave him a new status in the eyes of other people. Boys watched him curiously and asked him interesting questions, and adults plied him with sympathy.

'Yes,' said Mr Ralph Porlock, 'I read of it in the newspaper.'

He poured beer steadily into his tipped glass. 'Are you very distressed?'

He looked up suddenly.

James Fount felt uncomfortable and did not reply.

'No,' said Mr Porlock, 'I think that you are not.'

'I'm sorry.'

'And how is this going to affect your future? Is there to be any change of plan?'

'I – I'm not sure. I don't know if there have been any plans for me.'

'Of course there have.'

'Oh.'

'I have made plans, I spoke of them to your mother some time ago. You are one of the best pupils it has been my good fortune to teach.'

James Fount flushed crimson.

'I have said nothing of that kind before and I do not believe I shall say it again, you are likely to become more conceited than most boys. But when you are thirteen, you should sit for a scholarship to a public school, and there you will specialize in music, take up another instrument.'

'I don't know – she might not let me. I wanted to do that before and she wouldn't let me.'

'*I* will speak to your mother. You are not a stupid boy, it should not be beyond you to get a scholarship, so that she will not be financially inconvenienced.'

James Fount was silent. He had thought about it all himself time and time again, and never believed that any of it might happen, and now he stood in the Long Gallery of Mr Ralph Porlock's house and listened to calm, sure talk about a scholarship.

Mr Porlock wound some string round and round his hand. 'Well? That is what you want, Fount? You have always told me that you would be a musician, and now I am telling you how to go about it. Now is the time to be making plans, you are eleven years old already.'

'Yes,' said James Fount. 'Oh yes! I shall go and ask my mother straight away, but she can't say no, can she? I don't see how she could say no if I could get a scholarship – she ought to be pleased, I think. She can go and see the Headmaster and it will be all arranged.'

He began to run the moment Mr Porlock opened the front door. When Schwartz was thirteen he would go to a boarding school, it had long been decided, and Schwartz was often talking about it. Now, thought James Fount, now it will be me, now *I* shall go away. He ran hard down the dark streets.

My husband has asked me to write to you [Deirdre Fount read], and I am sure that you will quite understand when I explain that he has a nasty attack of gastric flu and really is not up to it himself. You will perhaps be surprised to know that Aubrey and I were married a fortnight ago, here in Birmingham.

He was very sorry to hear about your mother's death and asks me to thank you for letting him know. He is quite happy to leave all the plans about James to you, since you have looked after him and know best. Under the circumstances, you see that it is best for him not to come and visit you and in any case, he is really rather poorly just at present.

Yours faithfully,
Miriam E. Fount

So I have nobody, thought Mrs Deirdre Fount, crumpling the letter up tightly in her hand, nobody to help me and offer strength and comfort. I am alone as never before.

'I shall not come down to the dining room tonight,' said Major Bertram Carpenter. 'Now do not frown and look alarmed, Flora, it will do me no harm to miss a meal.'

'But they will send something up for you on a tray, something nice and light so that you do not have your indigestion. Perhaps a soufflé?'

'No, no. I shall take my medicine and go early to bed.'

'Then *I* shall not go down, they can send up a tray for me.'

Major Carpenter looked about for his spectacles. How little I can do for him, thought his wife, how vulnerable he is. I would give anything at all for this threat to be done away with. I would rather it had been me, for I should know better how to cope.

'You are being difficult, Flora.'

'I am only thinking of you.'

'Well do not, I am happy for you to think for yourself. You enjoy your dinner in the company of all the other guests, for it gives you a chance to look about you, and be inquisitive, talk to all kinds of people. *I* do not enjoy that sort of thing but you find it entertaining, so you have told me. Do not be a martyr on *my* behalf.'

Mrs Flora Carpenter sighed. He will become very tetchy, she thought, very difficult, if this illness progresses.

'Well, if you are quite sure, dear . . .'

For he was right, she did love the time of changing her frock and going down to the dining room, and perhaps making new friends in the coffee lounge afterwards.

'The matter is settled, you are going down to dinner alone and I am going to bed, and there is an end, Flora. We should have learned to say what we mean to one another, by now, to be entirely straightforward.'

But of course we have not, he thought, we are both acting a lie, both trying to conceal something of importance for the good of the other. We have been married for fifty years and neither of us can be sure of what the other is thinking.

'I hope that is settled,' said Major Carpenter aloud.

'Oh yes. Yes, of course, dear, if that is what you want. Quite settled.'

Mrs Carpenter went to take her bath, before dressing for dinner.

'You are being very unkind to me, James. I think you are old enough to understand that, by now. Your grandmother has not long died and I am suffering from shock. There is everything to be done here, so much work, I wonder how I shall be able to manage, and I have been left suddenly alone. You are all I have now, yet you come racing in here full of talk about winning scholarships and going away to a boarding school. It is very unkind and inconsiderate.'

James Fount sat on the cane chair and looked across at his mother.

'Why am I? I don't see why I am.'

'How do you expect me to give my mind to all these things now? I never thought I had borne a son who was insensitive to the feelings of others, even to those of his own mother.'

She sounds like my grandmother, thought James Fount, and I

wish she would not say those kind of things to me. But he knew what it was he wanted, now, and also knew that he would get it. Looking at her across the counter, he felt neither guilty nor uncomfortable.

'Mr Porlock says I'm good enough, he says I can *easily* get a scholarship. You wouldn't have to *pay*, or not very much, anyway.'

Mrs Fount stiffened. 'I am quite able to provide for you, James, we are not *poor*. Because you have made friends with Mark Schwartz, whose family show off their money while we live quietly, does not mean that we have no resources. Your grandmother left me quite enough on which to live comfortably *and* pay for any school fees.'

'But I'd still have to go in for the entrance exam and you have to put your name down soon.'

'You are not yet twelve. I do not see that there is any need to think and fuss about it at present.'

'But you've got to tell the Headmaster and he can apply. Schwartz is going and he knows all about it. But he wouldn't do music. I shall. I shall have to go somewhere that does music most of all, but it's all right, because Mr Porlock will tell me, he knows all about it.'

'It is very upsetting, James, I *really* do not think you can understand how I feel, standing here and listening to you planning your own future away from me and talking as though everything was agreed, as though you were going away tomorrow.'

'I wish I was,' said James Fount.

I will not be angry, she thought, I will not even appear to be very upset by that, though he *has* upset me, with his careless talk. For there must be a reason and I have a duty to discover it, and help him as best I may. Perhaps this is his way of showing the grief he feels at his grandmother's death.

'Why are you unhappy, dear?' she asked, therefore.

'I'm not.'

'Oh now, come. You can tell *me* about it. What is it that has upset you?'

'I'm all right.'

'I thought you were happy at Westbourne Priors.'

'I am. I like it for now, but I just don't want to stay on and on, do I?'

'Why?'

'Because I want to go away. I want to do music.'

'You do music now.'

'Not the same. I mean *really*.'

'But do you not think that you might feel rather lost in a new school, among lots of strange boys? You have never been away from home before. Might you not be *very* unhappy?'

'No,' said James Fount.

'Then I do not think you have really thought about it.'

'I have, I've thought about it all the time, it's what I've always wanted to do.'

Deirdre Fount was silent. He has a stubborn face, she thought, I have never really noticed that until now. He is self-willed and headstrong, and I cannot think what I have done to make him so. Whatever I say, his mind is set and I shall never change it. He will go away.

Aloud, she said, 'I cannot talk about it any more just now, James, it is far, far too soon and I am far too busy. There is a great deal to consider. I think I know more about it than you do and I am the one who is responsible for your future. You are still a child, although I am sure that eleven seems a very grown-up age to you.'

James Fount got off the cane chair and picked up his satchel. 'I'm going to tea with Schwartz,' he said.

'I *beg* your pardon? How dare you tell me what you are or are not going to do, without so much as asking my permission.'

'I'm sorry. May I go to tea with Schwartz?'

'Oh go on, go on, do what you like, I do not care for you. You have more feeling for your friend Schwartz and his family than you have for me.'

James Fount left the shop.

I am saying all the things to him that I vowed I would never say, thought Mrs Fount. I am becoming more and more like my own mother was with me and I cannot help myself, for now I understand. I see it all and I am miserable and afraid.

Across the street James Fount met his friend Schwartz.

'It'll be all right,' he said.

'Did she say it was? Did she say you could?'

'No. But she will. In a bit. It'll be *quite* all right.'

The two boys walked off together.

After dinner, Mrs Flora Carpenter sat in the Red Lounge and started to make conversation with the wife of a retired Archdeacon, a Mrs Plessy from the Channel Islands. Mrs Plessy had a grand-daughter lately married, and brought out colour slides, and Mrs Carpenter talked of Edward and the boys, and felt gay.

'It is quite a treat for me,' she confided, 'to sit here and relax a little and not feel guilty. My husband is slightly cross-tempered these days, he has not been too well and a close friend died suddenly. He does get rather annoyed if I stay behind chatting to anyone but I simply love it, I meet so many new guests and that is one of the delights of living in a hotel.'

Mrs Plessy nodded. In the end, it was almost eleven o'clock before they left the Red Lounge.

That was exactly what I needed, thought Mrs Carpenter, some new and friendly company. I hope we shall have a lot of time together while they are staying here. I feel so much more cheery, all of a sudden, even rather hopeful. Bertram will be quite envious, but I shall not wake him and talk at this hour, it can all wait until morning.

Major Carpenter was not in bed. He lay on the sofa, turned a little on his side and with a rug half-pulled up over his knees. His spectacles lay beside him on the floor. While his wife had been talking to Mrs Plessy in the Red Lounge, he had suffered a coronary thrombosis and lost consciousness very quickly, even before he thought to call for help.

Now, Mrs Flora Carpenter leaned over him and touched his forehead and knew that he was dead.

Chapter Thirteen

'I HAVE made up my mind,' said Mrs Auriole Carpenter to her husband, a week after the funeral. 'I will not have anyone say that I do not know where my duty lies.'

Edward Carpenter looked down the list of evening television programmes, and felt depressed.

'I will write to your mother and invite her to come here.'

He raised his eyebrows.

'For a few weeks, at least. *Three* weeks, I think, that seems fair. It will be long enough to make the journey worthwhile, and not long enough for us to get on top of one another. There is no use my promising to *try* having her live with us permanently, Edward, because I have seen that situation time and time again and it always makes for unhappiness. When the boys are at home it would be even worse. You know that your mother is wickedly indulgent with them. No, no, I hope you will not think me harsh, but I cannot agree to have her live with us.'

'Nobody has asked you to agree to it,' said Edward Carpenter. 'Not to my knowledge. I certainly have not.'

'No ...'

'Has my mother spoken to you?'

'She has not said anything directly, she has not exactly *asked*, but I could tell that I was expected to make an offer, she was talking about the future and hints were dropped.'

'My mother never hints.'

'Well, *I* think we should invite her for some weeks, whatever you say.'

'Yes, I am perfectly happy about it.'

'She will be able to get over the worst of the shock and pull herself together a little. I thought she was looking rather poorly.'

'Did you? It seemed to *me* that she was surprisingly well – better, indeed, than for some time.'

Mrs Auriole Carpenter looked up sharply. 'I do not think that is a very nice observation, Edward, you are not very sensitive. I am sure *I* have been very upset by your father's death, and I am not the one who was married to him for over fifty years. But I will write to her and be very sympathetic, and I will show her that she is wanted here, at least for a week or two, that we are trying to do our best for her.'

Edward Carpenter rose and switched on the television set for a comedy programme.

'We are so glad to see you, my dear, it is so good of you to come,' said Miss Violet Prug. And Mrs Christie began to pour out small glasses of sherry.

'I promised myself that we should entertain you one evening, soon. I did not think it at all necessary to hold back until anything like a "decent interval" might be supposed to have passed. Because it is *now* that you will be in need of your friends. It is not as though we were asking you to be gay, just to have a little supper with friends, which will do you the world of good and take you out of yourself. I do not ever feel quite comfortable if I know that there is someone lately bereaved, in need of a little company, an evening out.'

'How kind, very kind!' said Mrs Flora Carpenter, a little flustered by such a long speech from Violet Prug, and all directed at herself.

Mrs Christie handed round the sherry glasses and then went back to her kitchen, thinking all the while of Mrs Deirdre Fount, who had lost her mother and never yet been invited here to supper.

In the sitting room, Mrs Carpenter, looking rather pretty in her black, said, 'But it was a blessing, really you know, a blessing,' and began to tell Miss Prug about the suspected cancer.

'The very first words I uttered,' she said, ' – and I hope you will not be shocked – the very first words were, "Thank God," – for I would not have had him suffer.'

But a little later, she brought herself to talk about what was really on her mind, for she had been worrying about it, anxious to do the right thing. Miss Prug offered her another Floris chocolate and looked most doubtful.

'But surely,' she said to Mrs Carpenter, 'it is only for a week or so, and you would be wisest to go. You need to have a little rest, to get your bearings.'

'I have never lost my bearings,' said Mrs Carpenter, 'I am altogether myself.'

'It has been a shock. You cannot deny that.'

'Oh yes. But after all these years, I think I know myself, I think I see how best I may get over it. But I do not want to hurt and offend my daughter-in-law, for it is so kind of her to offer. I know that she does not enjoy having guests in the house. Perhaps they have only invited me because they feel it is their duty, they have made the gesture.'

'Oh, now ...'

'Yes, perhaps I am judging harshly, you may be right. But in any case, I shall not go, I am determined to stay in Westbourne. This is my home and here are my friends.'

'Of course you will be well looked after in the hotel. You have no worries or that score.'

Mrs Flora Carpenter smiled. 'Oh, but I do not intend to stay on in the hotel for very much longer, she said. At the beginning of the spring, when the weather is warmer, I shall leave.'

'Leave the Prince of Wales Hotel? Oh, my dear, I do beg you to think very carefully! If they have not been as efficient as they should, if things are wrong in some way, then complain, complain bitterly, but I really do not think that you will find any other hotel in this town up to the same high standard, I do not ...'

'Ah, I shall not go to another hotel. No. You see, although I have been very happy there, I have enjoyed myself among the guests and so on, really it was Bertram who was so determined to move in there, he wanted to give up the house and live permanently in a hotel. I agreed for his sake, and I do not say that I have been unhappy there. But it is time for a change.'

'Then what will you do? Whatever will you do?' Miss Violet Prug sounded most alarmed.

'I shall buy a flat!' said Mrs Flora Carpenter. 'A flat in the new block at the upper end of the Esplanade. They are to be luxury flats, you see, with full service and central heating, every possible comfort. *That* is what I shall do.'

Miss Prug shook her head. She herself had often thought of giving up her own flat and moving, like the Carpenters, into a hotel.

'I hope you will forgive me,' she said therefore, 'but is it quite wise to think of taking on a flat at your time of life? There will be so much to do, so many things to worry about, though I imagine you will have someone like my Mrs Christie, of course – a companion, a housekeeper.'

'I shall have someone to do my cleaning,' said Mrs Carpenter, 'that is all. And I shall eat out a good deal, I daresay, I shall go a lot to the Prince of Wales Hotel. But I am not so very old, Miss Prug, I am only seventy-one and very healthy. I have years ahead of me, I have no excuse for being a burden to others.'

'Yes, yes . . .'

Mrs Carpenter leaned forward a little, towards the fire.

'I will not give way to old age and death,' she said in a firm voice, 'I will not go into a decline and live off the kindness of others, because I am now a widow. No, I have quite decided to take myself in hand *at once*. I shall fill my life very full, Miss Prug, it is the only way to help me bear the loss of my husband. I shall have my own flat and my own furniture about me and I shall start to live a social life again, entertain my friends and have guests to stay. But I do not want to spend every day looking for ways of passing the time and diverting myself, so I have decided to find a little voluntary work, perhaps do something with the hospital, you know, or children's charities. I have not yet looked into it fully. But I am a rich woman, after all, and there must be a great deal for me to do.'

'You will overdo things, Mrs Carpenter, you will tire yourself out with a round of entertaining and helping others. Moving into a new flat alone will give you more than enough to do.'

'No, no. Bertram would never have wanted me to sit back and mourn and live a twilight existence, he himself was always active and full of vigour.'

But how easy it is to talk, she thought, how easy to decide what others would or would not have wanted, after they are dead and cannot contradict us. *I* do not know what Bertram would have wanted. We lived together for over fifty years and I never knew his mind. Really, I am doing what I please, I am going to live the sort of life I think I should enjoy and perhaps he would say that it is most foolish. But I have spent so long, ever since I was only a girl following in the wake of my husband, trying to think of him and make him happy, for that was my duty, and I was happy to do it. I have just now begun to realize that I do not know what it means to stand up alone and be independent, and that is an experience everyone should have before they die.

'It is only a fortnight, after all,' said Miss Violet Prug to her companion, after Mrs Carpenter had gone. 'I hope she will not go making any rash decisions yet awhile. It is all very well to talk of a new life and independence, of entertaining and helping others, but she can have no real idea of what that entails, none at all.'

'But, if it keeps her happy,' said Mrs Christie mildly.

'I only hope we do not see her come to grief. It is far too soon to be talking about all these changes, she has not had time to take in the fact of her loss.'

'Not,' said Mrs Christie, 'like poor Deirdre Fount, who is going about like some lost soul. She has been quite bemused by *her* bereavement.'

Miss Prug began to propel her wheelchair across the sitting room. 'I must remember to do something about Mrs Fount,' she said, 'I must remember to have her to tea. Now, I think I should like to take a bath, dear, if you will be so kind as to help me.'

If I sold this shop, thought Deirdre Fount, I could take a really proper holiday, before deciding on my new life. I could go on a cruise, to the Canary Islands, or the Bahamas or South Africa. James wishes to go away to a boarding school – very well, then, he could be sent now, as soon as possible and I could be off. I would meet plenty of new people and see all the countries I have longed to see.

She sat on the tall stool behind the counter, her hands resting on the cards of yarded lace and broderie anglaise edging that she had been rearranging. I would sit all day on the first class deck, she thought, in the sunshine. White coated waiters would serve cold drinks and people would wave and shout to me from the swimming pool, the day would be full of pleasures, there would scarcely be time for them all, and in the evening we would dress for dinner.

But not yet, she thought, re-winding the scalloped edging, not for a while, for my mother has not long been gone and I am by no means recovered, it would be very foolish to start making major changes and decisions while I am still in a state of shock.

Besides, James is not old enough to go away yet, it will be time enough when he is thirteen, *then* I shall see. But not yet. And if I sold the shop I might never find another to build up into a good business like this, I might regret it bitterly and lose a great deal of money.

No, I am better off at home, for the moment I will stay among friends here in Westbourne. She looked up and saw Mrs Flora Carpenter pass the window. Now here is someone else, thought Deirdre Fount, who has suffered a sudden loss, here is someone who understands what it is like to be quite alone. Perhaps she has come here for comfort and sympathy, perhaps she has come to invite me to dinner at the Prince of Wales Hotel.

'I have come to buy a lot of new embroidery silks,' said Mrs Carpenter. 'I want something a little out of the ordinary, and some metallic thread, too, gold and copper and silver. I do hope you can find me some.'

Deirdre Fount was shocked, for Mrs Flora Carpenter seemed quite gay.

'I have just enrolled for modern embroidery classes,' she said now, 'at the Technical School. I have been looking at all their lovely things, you know, and realizing just how old-fashioned my ideas must be. Well, it will do me good to learn something quite new, it will open a whole new world of interests, I expect.'

Deirdre Fount bent down to lift out the drawers of silks. It is not right, she thought, listening to Mrs Carpenter's enthusiasms, it is unseemly for her to come in this shop so full of excitement, looking so well and happy, when her husband is not three weeks dead. Grief should be concealed a little in public, that is only right, but I must say that Mrs Carpenter does not look as though she has suffered any grief at all.

For she did not know of Mrs Carpenter's resolution about a new and active life, did not know of the long nights when she lay awake in her room at the Prince of Wales Hotel and thought of how her husband had died. He was alone, she said to herself, a hundred times a day, he was alone, there was nobody to help. He died alone. At night, Mrs Flora Carpenter wept, but she said nothing about any of it aloud, nothing to anyone.

'*I* do not intend to start making many changes,' said Deirdre Fount now, 'I feel it is my duty to stay on here. Partly of course, because this is my home, it is what I am used to, and partly for James's sake. But I do feel that it is what my mother would have wanted. I am carrying on the shop, as it has always been, because that is what she would do in such circumstances. I would not dream of running away, breaking all ties and destroying the business she worked so hard for.'

Mrs Carpenter took her change and her parcels and left the shop sadly. She is very young, she thought, not yet forty, and already she has given in, she is afraid of life, she will have nothing to look forward to in the future. Well, that shall be a warning to me, a reminder, for if I do not put on a brave face and show the world that I am making some effort to live my life independently, people will soon tire of me, I cannot expect for more than a little friendship and company from time to time. People have their own lives to lead. *My* future is entirely up to me. And she set herself against the east wind and in the direction of the Upper Esplanade, where the new luxury flats were being erected.

On the cliff path, the girl Yvonne stood with her hands in the pockets of her sensible tweed coat and stared out to sea. Aubrey, she thought, Aubrey . . .

Behind her, lights began to go on in the rooms of Westbourne. At the back of the shop, Deirdre Fount made herself a pot of tea and began to wonder about the ordering of new light-weight wools in time for the spring.